VOICES FROM THE DARK

*Dan Mallett Investigations
Book Eight*

Roger Longrigg
writing as
Frank Parrish

SAPERE
BOOKS

VOICES FROM THE DARK

Published by Sapere Books.

20 Windermere Drive, Leeds, England, LS17 7UZ,
United Kingdom

saperebooks.com

ISBN: 978-1-80055-135-0

CHAPTER 1

It was strange to be alone in somebody else's house in the middle of the afternoon. It was normal perhaps for a burglar or a squatter, but it felt strange to Pippa Lees, even after five days in that house, even though she had the dogs there.

It was strange and frightening because of footsteps in the dark, and peculiar telephone calls, and unseen people coming and going.

Pippa should never have come. Having come, she should have left. But she was a prisoner of the promises she had made.

Pippa was there to look after the house, and the birds and the animals, while the owner was away. She was to push the trip-switch if the lights fused. There were precautions to take in a hard frost, and greenhouse skylights to open on a warm midday. There were indoor plants to water, the dogs to walk and feed, horses to bring in and out, bantams in a hayloft and little birds in an aviary. None of it was very taxing. It passed the time. Certainly somebody had to be there. The job Pippa was doing was normal. Hundreds of people did it, regularly or occasionally. But Pippa had never done it before, and she found it lonely and unnerving. It was strange to live in a house so lived-in without really knowing the people who lived there. She felt like an intruder, a trespasser; she felt she must whisper when she called the dogs, and walk through the rooms on tiptoe.

Pippa walked the dogs at two thirty, keeping Jake the dachshund on the lead but letting the other two run. The springer was too old to be bothered to run away or to chase anything, and the King Charles puppy too affectionate to want to run away.

It was cold but not freezing, the air damp, the sky colourless except when briefly illuminated by a flare of golden sunshine, which splashed across the ploughland and the grass and the winter wheat, and the dark tangled woods of the river valley, sun with no warmth but containing a kind of promise. It was only a week into the new year. The old year had ended for Pippa as badly as could be. The pale flares of sunshine across the landscape promised better things, and so did the exuberant love of Mr Tomkins, the King Charles spaniel.

A great congregation of lapwings strutted and flapped on a twenty-acre oblong of maize stubble, bullied by a handful of gulls. The neighbouring pastures were speckled by mixed flocks of fieldfares, redwings and thrushes. Among the brittle weed-stems in a hedgerow, two tiny goldcrests were hunting for the eggs of insects. Under the miles of cold clay it was beginning to be possible to imagine life reawakened.

The day was darkening quickly by the time they got back to the house. It was time to deal with the horses. Pippa got the feeds ready in the mangers in the three looseboxes. Scoops of oats, bran and nuts. From the loft she dropped bricks of hay into the racks. She filled three buckets from the standpipe and put them in the boxes. She took three halters off their pegs in the tack-room, knowing they were probably unnecessary, and went out into the paddocks. The horses came to her long before she could get to them. They ambled past her towards the stable. She did not need the halters, nor to push the animals into the right boxes. They knew it was teatime and they knew where to go.

The bantams returned to their roosts in the hayloft. They chuckled to one another, or to the horses, or to Pippa.

It was dark indoors. Pippa walked about the house, turning on lights. She drew curtains. She filled and switched on the electric kettle in the kitchen. She sat drinking tea at the kitchen table. The dogs came into the kitchen and told her it was time for their supper, but it was a try-on and they all knew it. They would be fed at six. An empty hour stretched ahead of Pippa until then, and after that an empty evening.

There were books in the big and small sitting-rooms, in all the bedrooms, and in shelves in the upstairs passages. Among all that lot there were bound to be books that would make her forget Fenton Lowell for a bit. There was a television and a radio. She could light a fire in either sitting-room, or sit in the kitchen, which was well-lit and warmed by the Aga. All those options. The thing was to be positive, to enjoy the quiet she had come for.

She fed the dogs a little early, because she could no longer endure the pleading in the eyes of Mr Tomkins, the King Charles puppy.

As on the previous evenings, it turned out to be difficult to find a book. Even among all those books there did not seem to be one she could bear the thought of reading. She was not in a mood to be easily pleased; perhaps she was not in a mood to be pleased at all. There were shelves of Dickens and Thackeray, of Trollope and George Eliot, but she did not want to reread the ones she had read, and she did not have the energy to embark on any of the ones she had not read, and in any case all those books were simply too big. In other shelves there were biographies and many books of history and travel, which would tell her more about their subjects than she wanted to know. She felt a great weariness when she thought of those billions of pages of print.

Meanwhile, it passed the time, to be looking at the spines of books.

Shortly after seven, the telephone rang.

'Hallo?'

'Hallo there,' said a man's voice which Pippa recognized. 'Is that the resident ray of sunshine?'

'Phillipa Lees speaking.'

'This is your friendly neighbourhood mystery man. Has there been any further communication from Mrs Marriner?'

'I haven't heard from her again.'

Jacob began his furious, frequent, high-pitched barking at a shadow of a sofa cushion. He was a really annoying little dog.

The man on the telephone, so it seemed to Pippa, said something about shutting the dachs up.

'What?' she said, startled.

'She does put people's backs up,' said the caller. 'I refer to Mrs Marriner. She is neglectful. She must know very well that you would be glad of a call.'

'Hmm,' said Pippa. What the man said was true, but she did not think it was any of his business.

'I'm sorry to keep disturbing you,' said the voice, which did not sound sorry at all. 'Bye-bye for now.'

'Goodbye,' said Pippa after a moment; but by that time the caller had hung up.

He had not said anything about Mrs Marriner putting people's backs up. He said something about shutting the dachs up. He heard the barking on the telephone, and he knew what kind of dog was barking. That was absolutely impossible unless he knew the house, knew the dogs. So he was a friend. In that case, why did he not identify himself? Why not leave a message? Pippa had not liked the sound of his voice when he first rang, the day of her arrival, and she still did not like it. It was a smooth voice. The speaker sounded as though he thought he was clever. He sounded knowing, and as though he had a sneer. He sounded creepy and insinuating. He knew the yappy little dog was a dachshund.

In her job, when she had a job, and in her private life, when she had one of those, Pippa had made and received many international telephone calls. She knew that, when things were right, modern technology put the person at the other end into the next room. 'The friendly neighbourhood mystery man', as he stupidly called himself, might be in California or Canberra. But Pippa had the clear, curious notion that he was very near at hand — not many miles away, not many hundreds of yards, just over the hill, perhaps, just down the road…

Perhaps it was not that he knew the household, but that he had been watching the house.

He did not sound like a friend. He sounded like anything but a friend.

Mrs Marriner had left a list of numbers of people that Pippa might need — the vet, the plumber and suchlike — but not a list of people who might ring up. How could she? There could not be such a list. Nobody could predict who would ring up. There was nothing by the telephone or on the desk to give any hint who this glib, this slimy-sounding caller might be.

Pippa did what she had not done before, not until bedtime; she went all round the house checking that the windows were securely latched and the three doors locked. She did not go into the annexe, the self-contained east wing of the house which was empty and locked up.

There was not really much need for elaborate precautions, not with a dog like Jacob in the house. The old springer might snuffle and snore and ignore an intruder, the spaniel puppy might slaver over the burglar's boots, but not Jacob. The most familiar and peaceable guest had to be protected from Jacob.

Even Jacob could not bite an unpleasant voice on the telephone.

Pippa put the remaining half of last night's casserole on the top of the Aga. She put on some sprouts which she had picked in the vegetable garden in the morning. There were potatoes in a sack in the back porch, but she decided she was better without them. In truth, she could not be bothered to peel and cook them. It was the sort of thing which was worth doing if there were two of you. She had bought some fruit the previous day, bananas and grapes and tangerines, extravagant but healthy; and there was plenty of cheese. That looked after dinner. It was not very interesting, but it was perfectly all right. She could have it on her lap, in front of the television in the small sitting-room, or she could sit with a book at the kitchen table.

Fenton had got her into the way of despising the television. She was not sure if watching it, or not watching it, would more keenly remind her of all that.

She wondered whether to have a drink. There was a bottle of Haig of which she had only had a couple of tots. The taste of Scotch would definitely remind her of Fenton; but then so would the taste of almost any kind of food, and the sound of any classical music. She could not go through life avoiding everything that reminded her of one treacherous lover.

She was deciding to have the drink when the dogs said they wanted to go out. It was Jacob's idea, as always. He was the one with the strong character. The others would hardly ever have gone out unless Jacob gave them a lead. Probably they did not really need to go out. It was a funny time. She would have expected them to go through until their last run at bedtime.

But she did not think she could call Jacob's bluff; she had only known him for a few days, and they were not her carpets.

She went into the back passage and opened the door on to the yard. She turned on the outside light as she did so. Jacob went out immediately, sniffing, listening, hurrying, a glossy, liver-coloured sausage-dog with his belly almost on the ground; Mr Tomkins the spaniel stumbled out, his feet and ears too big for the rest of him, with an air of doing this only out of loyalty; old Bunbury the springer sighed as he went out, humouring Jacob and Pippa both.

Pippa paused in the open doorway to sniff the night. There was no wind. It was colder. In the light from the back door and from the uncurtained windows of the passage, she crossed the yard to the stable. She got the three stable-rugs out of the tack-room, and spread them over the backs of the horses. She buckled the webbing surcingles over the rugs. The horses were sleepy, apathetic. Pippa did not think they wanted the rugs, but she thought they would want them at four in the morning.

She turned off the lights in the stable and bolted the outer door. She stood for a moment, listening.

From the darkness two hundred yards away, the edge of the wood beyond the garden, the tawny owls were noisily telling one another how hungry they were, *ki-wack, ki-wack*, as though to warn all the little soft animals to hide under the roots of the trees. Little owls were also calling from another direction, louder, demanding attention, *cu-cu-cu*, a cry which would be heard a great way off.

Jacob barked once from the bottom of the drive. He might go out onto the road. There was no traffic. On a windless night like this, Pippa would have heard the engine of a car. She would have seen the flare of headlights on the trees. But it was strange that Jacob should bark only once. Even on brief acquaintance, Pippa knew him for a dog who went on barking once he had started, until he was convinced the danger had passed. But this time it was one yap and then silence. Pippa was nearly sure it was Jacob who had barked.

She went back to the house. Bunbury and Mr Tomkins were there, waiting by the back door to be let in. Mr Tomkins waved his plumy tail in greeting and jumped up and scrabbled with adoration at Pippa's corduroys. Bunbury allowed his ears to be pulled, but he was not a demonstrative dog. There was no sign of Jacob.

Pippa whistled. She called, 'Jake! Jake, come here, boy!'

Nothing had been said about Jacob going hunting, wandering off from the garden. He sometimes went off after hares and roe deer, but only when he could see them, only in daylight.

'Oh, damn the dog,' said Pippa out loud.

She was cold. She was alarmed about Jacob. She could not understand that single bark. She did not want to go on standing out of doors in the freezing darkness, nor leave the door open. Jacob had always come in with the others, in Pippa's experience of them — he usually led the others in, as he led them out.

If Jacob had found a fascinating smell at the bottom of the drive he would be barking his head off, like any good hound. A badger? His ancestors had been bred to hunt badgers, but not in silence. A fox? A prowling dog-fox was perfectly likely, and they were animals that every dog could smell. But Jacob would be barking like a mad thing. And if somebody had set a snare by the gate, or if he had caught his ears in a bramble or a twist of old barbed wire, good God, Pippa thought, he'd bring the sky down. What, then? One bark and silence. Why? Where was he?

'Jake! Come here, Jakey, here boy...'

The other dogs went past her, and along the passage to the kitchen. Bunbury would stretch out under the table, in the way of anybody sitting there, and Mr Tomkins would be in his beanbag. Jacob, if he was there, would somehow slither himself up into the little armchair in the corner; he did not seem to jump, but somehow crawled vertically upwards. Thinking of this, Pippa felt a great jolt of affection for the dog, of worry, of guilt.

Had she been careless, irresponsible? Had she done something wrong? Judith Marriner would think so.

Pippa called and whistled. She got the big flashlight from the pantry; she quartered the lawn, the vegetable garden, the shrubbery, the orchard, calling and whistling, stabbing and flailing at the darkness with the white beam of the flash.

She had come out of the house without gloves. Her fingers were too cold to work the switch of the flashlight. Jacob was not in the garden or the orchard, or the paddock or the wood. Pippa searched the stable, the looseboxes and the feed-store and the saddle-room, in case he had somehow slipped in with her. The horses shifted and sighed. There was no sign of Jacob in the stables, or in the garage or tool-shed. She began to be certain that it was useless to go on whistling and calling, but she thought she must go on trying.

She went indoors at last, freezing and despairing. She wondered what to do.

As she went from the back passage into the front hall, she passed the door of the downstairs cloakroom. She remembered she had left a pair of sheepskin mittens in there. She went in, turning on the light. It was typical of the downstairs loos of very many country houses Pippa had seen: the loo proper in a little box of a room beyond, and before that a kind of ante-room with a wash-basin and a wardrobe and a multitude of pegs, the last festooned with mackintoshes, shooting-coats, cartridge-belts and creels. The walls of the ante-room were covered in group photographs, of a kind seldom seen in any other kind of room — club and school and regimental photographs, the people dressed up to play cricket or go on parade, smiles on some faces and expressions of lunatic blankness on others. None of these photographs was new. None was less than forty years old, Pippa thought. The Bullingdon group was of 1935, and the officers arranged in tiers outside their mess had glared at the Aldershot camera in 1938.

Had Mrs Marriner's husband never belonged to anything?

Over the wash-basin hung a large, cloudy mirror in a chocolate-brown Victorian frame. Taken by surprise by the mirror, Pippa came face to face with her reflection.

For somebody who felt as she felt, she looked amazingly healthy.

She was twenty-six but, pink and dishevelled from rushing about outside in the cold, she looked eighteen, even fifteen. She had short fair hair, blue eyes, rather a long face, a long slender neck. Her face was never quite plain and often almost beautiful. She had been told that she looked her best when her face was animated, excited, but she had no way of knowing if this were so — when you were excited, you were not usually looking in a mirror, and when you were looking in a mirror you were very rarely excited. She was of medium height, slim, with an excellent figure, though that was invisible in the big baggy sweater she was wearing.

Her own reflection held her for a second.

She looked pretty good, pretty nice. A bit too wholesome, perhaps, for some tastes — she would have liked a touch of evil or decadence, but as far as she could see she had no trace of these fascinating things.

How on earth had she come to captivate a sophisticated cosmopolitan like Fenton Lowell? She had not set out to do so. It would never have occurred to her to try. She had done so. At least, she seemed to have done so. She had not done so for long. That was one of the reasons she was here.

Another reason was Jacob. Jacob, Jacob, where in God's name was Jacob?

Pippa whistled and called from the kitchen door and from the middle of the lawn. The beam of the flashlight skewered innumerable imitation Jacobs, shadows and tree stumps which made her heart jump with joyful relief and then sag into deeper despair.

Could he conceivably have wriggled in between her legs, or under cover of the others? No, but still she searched the house meticulously from bottom to top and down again, because she would have looked and felt such an awful fool if he had been indoors all this time...

The road. He never ran out on the road, but perhaps that was what he had done.

Pippa took the flashlight and the sheepskin mittens. She made sure she had the Yale key of the kitchen door. She made sure the other dogs were indoors. She pulled the door shut so that it locked, and went out to her car. It coughed to life, and she backed it out of the garage. She drove very slowly down the drive, searching once again the sides of the drive in the headlights. She turned out onto the road. There were no other cars. She went slowly westwards for a mile, searching the nearside verge in the headlights, and then back, searching the other verge. She went for a mile eastwards. She did not expect to see Jacob and did not do so.

She found that she was praying when she got back to the front courtyard of the house and to the yard at the back; praying that she would see a little slithery liver-coloured form with a sharp nose and a tail like a whip, that she would hear the volley of yapping barks which Jacob used to express every emotion…

Pippa stood outside the house whistling and calling, although it was obvious by now that this was useless. She felt sick with dismay.

She turned back towards the house. From where she stood she could see the windows of the back passage and of the kitchen, and of the downstairs loo. The kitchen and the passage were brightly lit, light from the uncurtained windows flooding out onto the cobbles of the back yard. In the light there were clouds of little grey winter moths, disturbed from the shrubs, perhaps, by Pippa's passing, looking immaterial, a product of the cold air or of tired eyes, tiny frail insects astonishing to see in a freezing night.

Lights in the kitchen, yes, in the back passage, yes. The door of the Gents open, and a little light filtering through its window into the yard, light from the passage reflected on the glass of those group photographs… But Pippa was certain she had shut the door of the Gents.

Why was she certain? She just was. Why had she shut it? She just had. A dog might have shut the door if she had left it open, but no dog could open the door if she had left it shut. Not even Jacob could have done that.

Pippa was frightened for Jacob. Now suddenly she was frightened for herself.

Frightened, she let herself in by the back door. Mr Tomkins rushed at her with adoration. She got the poker from the fireplace in the small sitting-room. She wanted Bunbury to come with her when she searched the house again, but he thought it was a stupid game; he rolled over and went back to sleep under the kitchen table. Pippa and Mr Tomkins searched the house. Pippa turned on all the lights in the house and left them all on. She thought it was not extravagant under the circumstances. There was no sign of there having been any intruder in the house. Mr Tomkins was neither more nor less excited than usual. Pippa had no idea what to think or to do.

She wondered if there was any connection between the disappearance of Jacob, the creepy voice on the telephone, and the opening of the door of the cloakroom. They all had in common that they were strange and frightening. It was too many strange and frightening things for one night. Pippa wished she had not come to this house.

She went down to the kitchen and found that the sprouts had boiled dry in their saucepan on the top of the Aga. They were burned. There was no other green vegetable, and the pan would be hell to clean. She supposed she had not smelled the burning because the lid fitted tightly. It was one other thing, it was one thing too many, it was too much. Pippa began to cry useless and childish tears, about Jacob and the burned sprouts.

She heard a car. The dogs heard it. Bunbury shifted his forelegs and opened one eye.

Hope came like a sunrise: it was somebody bringing back Jacob. The local people knew these dogs. Rather than telephoning they had simply arrived.

Pippa went through the house to the front door, but as she reached it she heard the knocker of the back door. She ran back, a kind of muddled prayer forming in her head as she ran. She threw the back door open.

A woman stood there, wearing a headscarf and a heavy tweed coat. It was Mary Craik, from Berryes, from the house the other side of the valley. She was carrying a bag and a pair of gloves.

'Oh,' said Pippa stupidly. 'I thought you might have Jacob.'

'Why in God's name would I have Jacob?' said Mrs Craik. 'Jacob, Jakey. Jack. Who have you got?'

'What do you mean? The other dogs are here.'

'May I please come in?'

'Yes, of course, I'm sorry.'

'Not here yet?'

'What?'

'He hasn't arrived yet?'

'Who? What do you mean?'

'Ah. You haven't been told. I wonder why not. You have another caller. I thought he would have got here by now. Don't let me interrupt you. Carry on doing whatever you were doing. Eating, I suppose, at this hour. Carry on eating. Personally, I'm too excited.'

Mrs Craik walked up and down the kitchen. She obviously was excited. Pippa thought she was a little drunk. She wore brilliant lipstick, startling in deep country on a freezing weekday evening. Her heavy nose was heavily powdered. She looked more than ever like one of the women in Pippa's aunt's photographs, out with the Pytchley Hunt before the war, hard-riding women in bowler hats and veils, adulterous fox-hunting women from the Shires with a lot of money from trade or manufacture. Mary Craik was one of them, or if she wasn't she was working hard pretending to be one of them. As a child Pippa had been frightened of such women, and she was frightened of them still.

'I couldn't meet him at home, could I?' said Mrs Craik, as though certain of Pippa's agreement. 'Have you got a drink in this place?'

'I'm afraid I haven't,' lied Pippa. 'I expect Mrs Marriner has, but the cellar's locked.'

'Oh well, we can get into it when he comes.'

'Who's coming? I don't understand.'

Mary Craik took off her headscarf. Her hair was very black, cut short, permed into such tight waves that she looked as though she was wearing a hairnet, as though she had just taken off her hunting bowler and would soon put it on again.

'Nobody you've met,' she said, belatedly answering Pippa's question. 'I did think he might have rung you up.'

'Somebody did ring up. A man. He didn't give a name.'

'I expect that was him. Have you been burning something? Ghastly smell.'

Mary Craik was extremely edgy. Suspense was almost bursting through the enlarged pores of her nose. She took off her big tweed coat and dropped it on one of the kitchen chairs. She was wearing heavy tweeds underneath as well, biscuit-coloured tweeds with thick red stockings and suede boots. She was not dressed for romance. For some reason, she looked older without her overcoat; she looked fifty; she looked as though her jet-black hair must be dyed.

She was not just edgy, she was on heat. The presence of the dogs, perhaps, put this phrase into Pippa's head. It was a bit disgusting, applied to a middle-aged woman, but it was exact. Mary Craik was almost shamelessly avid to meet the man she was meeting.

Her lover? How could she possibly have a lover?

She had a secret and guilty relationship. Was that possible — a woman who looked like that, with manners and a personality like that? She could not meet her boyfriend in her own house, because she had a tough and dangerous husband. She met him here, in Judith Marriner's house. This was possible because Judith Marriner was away.

But Pippa was not away. She would see the lover. Probably she would hear his name. If anything happened, in bed or wherever, she would know about it. Didn't that matter to them? Didn't they care? They must assume she would tell Judith Marriner about all this. Didn't they care about that? What kind of people were these?

Mary Craik was not being coy about her assignation. Quite the contrary — she was practically boasting about it. She was boasting to a pretty young girl that she had an active and exciting sex-life. That was the way it seemed to Pippa.

'Are you sure you haven't got a drink?' Mary Craik said. 'If I'd known, I would have brought something.'

Pippa made a gesture of apology. She was not going to share her whisky with this horrible woman. She could not think of anything to say. She did not understand what was going on, why Mary Craik was doing something in secret, in such a way as to make sure it was not secret. She was worried sick about Jacob. Worry might have taken away her appetite, but in fact she was ravenous after hunting up and down in the freezing darkness. She did not want to eat under Mary Craik's eye. She thought that would give her indigestion.

Mr Tomkins, on the bean-bag, raised his head and pricked his ears. He had heard something Pippa had not heard. Mary Craik saw this also and stood still, listening.

It was a bark. It was Jacob's bark from outside, from somewhere off in the darkness.

'Oh my God,' said Pippa. She tried not to be too relieved, too elated, in case the bark was not Jacob's.

'You go and find him,' said Mrs Craik. 'It's too bloody cold for me.'

Pippa mumbled something, grabbed the flashlight and ran out of the back door. She stood listening. 'Jacob? Jakey?'

He barked again, a volley of yaps indignant or excited. He was down at the bottom again, near the gate at the end of the drive.

'Coming,' shouted Pippa.

She ran across the yard and started down the drive.

She thought she heard, as she went, the telephone ringing inside the house.

The beam of the torch was answered by two tiny golden searchlights. Jacob yapped and danced. He was in a state. He was excited and furious. Pippa saw that he was tied to the gatepost. He was wired to it. One end of the wire was twisted round the wood, the other round Jacob's collar. Jacob was wriggling and bouncing and barking, so that it was very difficult to get at the twisted wire. Pippa crooned to him and stroked him, feeling a sunrise of thankfulness. He did not want her caresses; he snapped impatiently; he wanted to be let off. Pippa tried to untwist the wire on his collar. In her sheepskin mittens it was impossible to grip the end of the wire. Whoever had done it had used a pair of pliers. Pippa took off her mittens and struggled with the wire with her bare hands. Very soon her hands were going to be too cold to cope with the wire. Jacob, wriggling, knocked over the flashlight, which she had propped on a stone on the ground.

Pippa needed pliers, but she could not bear to leave Jacob alone in the dark wired to the gatepost while she went to the tool-shed to fetch them. She struggled with the wire. The wire hurt her fingers. It was more and more painful as her fingers got colder. She heard herself whimpering. Jacob was snapping and wriggling and making everything ten times more difficult.

Pippa tried the other end of the wire, the gatepost end, but it was even more viciously twisted and enwrapped. She went back to the collar. Her fingers were freezing and bleeding. Her knees were hurting from kneeling on the frozen gravel of the drive.

Pippa released Jacob. He sped off ungratefully into the darkness. Terrified of losing him again, she whistled and called. She hurried up the drive, stiff, with sore knees and freezing and bleeding fingers.

As she went, she began to wonder who in God's name could have caught Jacob, and been prepared with pliers and two yards of wire, and why such a cruel and strange action, and what this had to do with all the other strange things of the night…

Jacob was barking furiously by the back door. He wanted to be let in out of the cold. That was obvious. Pippa wondered why Mrs Craik had not let him in. She might be excited and drunk, but surely she could get as far as the back door to let in a little dog?

Pippa opened the door, and Jacob popped into the house. He slithered on the linoleum of the kitchen floor. He made a lightning tour of the kitchen, acknowledging the other dogs.

Pippa wondered where Mrs Craik had got to. Then she remembered hearing the telephone. The nearest extension was in the small sitting-room. As a near neighbour, Mrs Craik probably knew that. Pippa went along the back passage, attended by Mr Tomkins. Nobody was talking on the telephone, as far as she could hear. Perhaps somebody on the other end was talking and talking, stopping her from letting the dog in.

Pippa paused outside the door of the room. There was no sound. Pippa was puzzled and a little nervous. She did not think the other expected caller could have arrived, unless he came a very funny way, but she did not want to break in on anything. She stood irresolute outside the door. Mr Tomkins decided for her. The door was ajar and he jumped up and pushed it open.

Mrs Craik was in the armchair by the desk, the telephoning armchair. She was sitting back in a position of extreme relaxation. Her head was in shadow. The telephone was beside her, its receiver in its cradle.

Approaching shyly, Pippa saw that Mrs Craik's eyes were closed. She was asleep. That was extraordinary. She had been so excited, agog to meet whoever was coming. She must have been much drunker than Pippa had realized. In her lap was a cushion from the other armchair. Why would she go to sleep with a big cushion in her lap? For comfort?

Mr Tomkins jumped into Mrs Craik's lap before Pippa could stop him.

'Down!' said Pippa. 'Get down! I'm sorry, he will do that...'

Mr Tomkins did not wake Mrs Craik up. He nuzzled her sleeping face with his nose, in affection and curiosity. Her head was nudged sideways a little. Her eyelids were closed and her hands motionless.

Pippa gave one small cry, and fell on her knees by the chair. She realized that Mrs Craik was dead. She saw that blood glinted wetly in the tight black waves on the top of Mrs Craik's head. She had been hit on the head. The poker was in the fireplace. There was blood on the poker. There was blood on the cushion in Mrs Craik's lap. Mrs Craik had been hit on the head with the poker, and then asphyxiated with the cushion while she was knocked out.

Mr Tomkins suddenly howled, as though he knew exactly what had happened.

CHAPTER 2

A zigzag trail had brought Pippa to this point.

Parsonage Farm, Medwell Fratrorum, not a parsonage nor a farm but a fourteen-room house of flint and brick, Georgian and Victorian, split into two unequal parts separately occupied, in five acres of mature garden, with five acres of paddocks additionally, stabling and other outbuildings; a place reached by dangerous lanes, with sharp corners and hedges halfway to the sky; a house on the rim of a river valley of unusual emptiness.

It was a house that should have been full, but was empty. It would have been a marvellous place for children, but there were no children.

Pippa was the only person — had been the only person — for many furlongs in any direction, and ever since her arrival she had been wondering if it was wise.

It had come about by the purest chance, but so pat to everyone's needs that it might have been planned. Pippa wondered if it had been planned, but she could not think by whom, or why, or how. She did not like the idea of being a puppet, or part of somebody's game of chess.

The arrangement might have seemed providential, but it was not so very strange. If Mrs Marriner had not found Pippa, she would have found somebody like her; and if Pippa had not found this position she would have found another like it, if the idea had occurred to her. After spending enough time on the telephone, Mrs Marriner would have found another competent, country-trained girl or a retired naval officer or a middle-aged couple temporarily homeless; after advertising in the *Country* magazine, Pippa would have found dogs and a house that needed looking after, in Cumbria or Cornwall.

A month before, Christmas on the horizon, Pippa had been living in the top-floor flat in the house of married friends in Battersea. She had an amusing job with an interior designer. She had an exciting American boyfriend; her relationship with him was possible because of the adult tolerance of the owners of the house where she lived, and the fact that her parents were in Indonesia. Probably if they had been at home she would still have had an affair with Fenton, but probably he would not have spent three nights a week in her flat. Pippa was five foot six. She was ash blonde and had recently had her hair cut short, so that her reflection often surprised herself. She was not one to stand out in a crowd by dint of her glamour or strangeness, but she was not one ever to be a wallflower. She was well educated but not highly sophisticated. She had been to an expensive school but not a university. She knew quite a lot about art but nothing about differential calculus. She was honest and housetrained and good with animals.

She did not know why Fenton Lowell had picked her, but she knew very well why she had picked him. He was thirty-eight, six foot one, buttercup-haired, hawkily handsome, with a high outdoorsy colour; he had a job that sometimes required sitting in front of a bank of screens in a city office, and sometimes jetting to Tokyo.

They had met with friends, a journalistic dinner party in Blackheath. He had started wooing her at once in a stately way, with flowers and theatre tickets. If he went back to New York, she would go with him. Meanwhile, they cooked pasta for one another, drank expensive red wine, and sometimes shared the bath in her flat.

Three bombs exploded during the month of December.

The couple who owned the house in Battersea split up. The wife packed up and went away with a most charming Dutchman. It was her money that had bought the house, so she felt entitled to leave it. It was to be put on the market, although the moment was a bad one. Pippa was not immediately evicted, but she had to begin urgently looking for something else she could afford. Properties were plummeting in value, but rents apparently not. She could not move in with Fenton, because his company had put him in a high-rent, high-security block with nosy porters.

This explosion on its own was tiresome but not disastrous. As long as she had a salary, she could have a roof over her head.

But Pippa's employer ran into cash-flow problems. He catered to the extravagant, so he was an early victim of the recession. He needed display in order to secure commissions, and commissions in order to finance display. He operated on margin, paying his bills only when he was paid. He had walked a financial tightrope for a number of years, but high interest rates puffed him off it into the safety net of bankruptcy. Pippa had no job.

That explosion on its own was still not so very terrible. Like the break-up of the marriage, it was inevitable in hindsight. There were other jobs. Pippa had a fair knowledge of her boss's trade. She was not on the breadline immediately, but it was difficult to be flat-hunting and job-hunting at the same time.

At short notice, Fenton was posted back to America. One day he was in London, the next day not. It was the way his company did things. They liked to discourage complacency in the staff, even at senior level; they liked to keep people on the hop.

For all of one shiny morning in the middle of December, all of Pippa's problems seemed to be solved in one stroke. She would go to New York.

One of his colleagues said to her, 'I can't understand how you didn't know, if you knew Fenton as well as you say. Sure he has a place in New York, a home to go to. He has an apartment on Central Park West. Of course he'll live there. He'll live there with his wife and two kids. Where else would the guy live?'

Fenton's wife would not travel. She would not take her children to live abroad. Her mother had a weak heart, and she would not live so far out of range of her. She did not want to sublet the precious apartment. She did not want to be separated from her friends. Any of these reasons would have served to keep her in New York, but she had all of the reasons.

Fenton's new London friends were as surprised as Pippa was. His old friends were only surprised that she did not know.

Pippa was suddenly disgusted with London. She was a country girl — what was she doing in a filthy city anyway? She wanted to get out. If she was running away, running away was what she was doing. Wounds needed licking, even if only for a couple of weeks. Pippa wanted trees and silence and nothing that reminded her of Fenton.

It would have been good to go abroad, but she could not afford to go anywhere hot at Christmas time. It was no fun going abroad alone, and nobody she could have endured as a companion could suddenly drop everything for a fortnight.

Pippa's mood was mixed. She was shattered and she was angry. She had been in love as never before, and she had been played with, made a fool of, suckered, betrayed. She had been ignorant and trusting and childishly romantic. She was hurt.

She tried to stoke her anger to drown out the pain, but it only worked for a minute at a time.

London taxis, the diesel thud, the astonishing manoeuvres, the cockney goodwill of the drivers — these were for Pippa the most potent reminders of Fenton, oddly; not bunches of carnations in the street or whisky sours or any music — not at first, although whisky and music carried a powerful charge. She had to get away from those London taxis. She had to get away from London.

Home would have been an option — rural Oxfordshire. But the house was let for two years to an Australian banker and his family. Even if her parents had been there, Pippa would probably not have gone home, to an atmosphere heavy with tact. Her mother would have been ready to listen, if she had wanted to confide; she would have been lavish with spoken and unspoken sympathy. Pippa mostly resisted crying, but at home she would have cried.

Other members of her family? She thought about them all. She reached a hand towards the telephone, and drew it back. Her aunts and uncles and cousins, her married sister, all had in this situation some fatal drawback or other. There were young cousins in Baldock who lived in a cheerful squalor for which Pippa already felt herself too old; they still acted like students, and burned holes in table tops with their cigarettes. There was an aunt who lived in the roaring centre of a big industrial town, and one who lived in gracious penury in a dripping and unheated house.

Pippa was devoted to her sister Catherine, and moderately fond of Catherine's husband, Rupert. But Rupert and Catherine were so draconically tidy that they made life a misery for anybody normal, and anybody normal made their lives a misery. You could not leave a newspaper on a table, or a book on the arm of a sofa. Pippa became exhausted with apologizing in that house, and Catherine with not reproaching her. It was no place to take a broken heart.

School friends? Friends of her parents? Oxfordshire neighbours? Pippa went through her address book.

There were people who knew nothing about Fenton or the flat or the job, and people who knew too much. There were many people who were too busy, and some who were not busy enough. There were those who would not sympathize enough, and those who would sympathize too much.

What was she to say? 'My heart's just been broken — my life is in pieces. Please take me in and have pity on me, and protect me from the sight and sound of a London taxi.'

You couldn't ask yourself to stay, in the country, just before Christmas, for no reason. Children would be coming home from school, and everybody would be busy and preoccupied. All right, perhaps, if there was a race-meeting in the vicinity — you could ask yourself for a weekend. You could ask yourself for a shoot, a dance, a christening, any colourable excuse. 'This is Philippa Lees. I hope you remember me? The thing is, my uncle's got a horse running next Saturday at Wincanton, and I wonder if possibly, if it's not frightfully inconvenient...'

It was only just possible, and in the run-up to Christmas it was less possible than at any other time.

And without such an excuse? Certainly there were people who would put her up for a few days, but their voices would be odd on the telephone, and they would look at her oddly when she arrived.

Licking wounds was one thing. Being publicly abject was another. Pippa had an urgent need to do something, and no idea what to do; a need to go somewhere, but nowhere to go.

In this state she allowed herself to be taken by her bankrupt boss to a private view in a gallery in South Kensington.

The pictures were worth a glance but not a second glance. They were done by a clever girl who was interested in making a living. They were all acrylics and nearly all stylized flower-pieces. They were not works of art but items for decorators. Pippa's two years in her job had given her an eye for such frauds, and the decor and lifestyle into which they were meant to fit. Fenton's flat was the sort of place in which these pictures belonged, although his own taste had been far different... *Bloody hell*, Pippa thought, *get out of my thoughts!*

She looked round for diversion, since she had seen enough of the pictures and her escort was not ready to leave. She found herself behind a thin woman, face invisible, with pale hair and a green silk suit.

'I thought you were just off to Rome, Judith?'

'I am, at least I was, but just at the moment I can't get away.'

'You always have before,' said the man she was talking to.

'Yes, but my tenant's just gone into hospital. There's got to be somebody there, especially at this time of year. All those damned animals.'

'People get people, I mean, there are people who come and housesit. People make a living out of doing it. One's always seeing their advertisements. Retired people. Widows. They'd beat a path to your door.'

'Not at short notice they won't. They're booked up. The ones people recommend are booked up months in advance. One can't throw the place open to just anybody, somebody without references, somebody who doesn't know about horses. I wanted to go immediately after Christmas, but now God knows when I shall get away.'

'Excuse me,' said Pippa. 'I couldn't help overhearing...'

Pippa had the use of her mother's Renault 5. Armed with directions (which after leaving the main road were most necessary), she drove down to Medwell. She arrived at the house at eleven thirty on a chilly Monday, a little late, the journey stretched by the puzzles of its last five miles.

She had to see if she could handle the place. Mrs Marriner had to be satisfied that she could handle it. There was much necessary briefing as to the watering of the cyclamen and the winding of the clocks. It was mostly familiar stuff to Pippa, although Parsonage Farm was grander than her parents' home.

Coming from London, you turned north two miles beyond a village with a big church and a pub and a single shop; you picked your way past isolated farms up a hill and down it, and then went along the rim of a valley. With good luck and good instructions you found white gates set in an enormous mixed hedge of hawthorn, hornbeam, lilac, snowberry and holly. A short drive curved between rhododendrons. Gaps revealed paddocks and post-and-rail fences, with two or three horses grazing in New Zealand rugs. Then you came to the house, with its front and back yards and its outbuildings.

The matter of references had been surprisingly easy, after a few minutes' conversation in the art gallery, and a few more on the telephone. Pippa's father's lawyer, who knew her family well, was known to a lawyer whom Mrs Marriner knew. Colleagues of Pippa's uncle, who was a brewer, were known to cousins of Mrs Marriner. Pippa's late boss had written an almost ridiculously glowing testimonial, motivated by guilt and loyalty.

There still had to be this inspection of the house by Pippa, and of Pippa by Mrs Marriner in the context of the house.

The occasion was a bit awkward.

Mrs Marriner came out of the house as Pippa climbed out of the car. The dogs came with her, a springer, a King Charles and a dachshund. The King Charles came wriggling forwards with instant adoration. He was a young puppy. The dachshund barked. The springer sat on the gravel, wondering if he could be bothered to scratch. He had the air of an old dog who knew that he ought to have become wise.

Seen here in the country, on a cold Monday morning, Mrs Marriner looked older and bleaker than in a warm London room in the evening. She was about forty. She was still tragically young to be a widow. Her husband had been drowned, so Pippa understood, his dinghy spotted off the Dorset coast capsized and empty. There were no children. They had only moved into this house shortly before the tragedy. It was a big house for one person, even though part of it was let.

The situation was clear cut. Mrs Marriner needed to get away for several days, to go to Italy for some pressing and private reason; but she could not do so unless somebody she could trust was left in charge. Lady Harrison, tenant of the rooms which constituted the east wing, was in hospital having a hip replacement. At her best, she could look after the birds and perhaps the dogs, but even at her best she could not have managed the horses.

'There's a local man who could cope with all the out-of-doors stuff,' said Mrs Marriner, 'but I haven't been able to get hold of him. He's not on the telephone, and when I go to his hovel I only find his old mother, who refuses to say where he is. Probably she can't say that or anything else. She's a deaf-mute, gaga, a pathetic dribbling old peasant. Probably, in point of fact, the son is in prison.'

'Is he often in prison?'

'Oh yes. In and out all the time. But he's useful here. He knows the place and the animals. He'll probably turn up here, out of the blue, to do something about the garden. He'll come to earn some money, when they let him out of prison. If he does come, don't let him into the house. Or, if you do, make him turn out his pockets before he leaves. And even then, count the spoons after he's gone.'

'Who is this bandit?' asked Pippa, laughing.

'He's called Dan Mallett.'

Dan Mallett. Pippa made a mental note of the name. It sounded like a folk hero, perhaps an American — Davy Crockett, Casey Jones, Will Rogers, it was that sort of name. Dan Mallett. It sounded like wood, a wooden tool, beech or yew, wood used by a craftsman, a wheelwright or cabinet-maker; it had a homespun, traditional, reliable ring.

But the owner of the name was a sticky-fingered jailbird, who lived with a senile dribbling mother in a disgusting hovel.

Dan Mallett. Pippa would remember and be on her guard.

'These won't give you much trouble,' said Mrs Marriner, waving at the dogs. 'Bunbury and Jacob, and the one you've got is Mr Tomkins.'

'I seem to have made a hit with Mr Tomkins.'

'Everybody makes a hit with him. He has no character or use or point. I've only got him because I was given him.'

Pippa thought this was a cold way to speak about a dog, but he did seem a very silly dog, without any dignity.

'You did say you were brought up with horses?'

'Yes. We had them at home. My sister and I always had ponies.'

'Did you belong to a thing called the Pony Club? I understand people do, or did.'

'Oh yes, we went to the camp year after year. We did hunter trials and show-jumping and all that…'

'You had a groom?'

'Oh no, we did it all ourselves. My mother is a tremendous expert.'

Again there was something chilly in the way Mrs Marriner spoke. It was as though she did not really care about the horses.

Mrs Marriner showed Pippa looseboxes, hayloft, feed-store and tack-room. It was solid and Victorian, weather-board above brick, with sloping cobbled floors. There was a standpipe nearby. The muck-heap was behind. There was a pitchfork, a shovel, a stiff broom and a set of grooming tools. There were half a dozen saddles of various sizes on trees, and tidy festoons of reins and bridles hanging from hooks on a beam. It was not glamorous, but it was workmanlike and cosy and familiar. After London, Pippa inhaled with delight the stable smells of her childhood.

She said, 'This is like coming home.'

Mrs Marriner glanced at her blankly. She did not look as though she knew what Pippa was talking about. The stables were not home to her. She was indifferent to all of this. If it was anything, it was a burden. Why did she have the horses? Three horses? They were something to do with the husband, they were his thing entirely? But he had been dead for three years. Were the horses kept as a kind of memorial? Or in case Mrs Marriner remarried a horsy man?

A flurry of blue-marble bantams came running to the rattle of corn in a scoop. Mrs Marriner showed Pippa where they roosted and where, even at that time of year, one of the hens might lay. The old springer was steady to the bantams, but the dachshund and the King Charles had to be restrained.

Mrs Marriner spoke impatiently about the mess the bantams made on the hayracks in the looseboxes.

Pippa thought: *if she keeps bantams, what the hell does she expect?*

Mrs Marriner did not really like the bantams. She was not interested in them. It was as though they were not her birds — as though she was responsible for them on a short-term basis only — as though she was looking after them for somebody else, conscientiously but without interest.

Was there nothing in the place Mrs Marriner did like?

Three or four fantail pigeons arrived with a whistle of pinions on the roof of the stable.

'We don't feed them,' said Mrs Marriner.

Pippa thought that, if the weather turned really cold, she would throw some corn to the fantails, in spite of Mrs Marriner's rules.

They toured the house, the nine rooms of the part which Mrs Marriner inhabited. It was a lot of house for one woman living alone. Two of the four bedrooms smelled damp and deserted — they were obviously never used. A third was quite a nice room, neat and characterless, a typical seldom-used guest-room. Pippa would sleep there if she came.

The master bedroom was large and luxurious. It belonged to Cadogan Square, not rural Wessex. Glossy magazines had been consulted, and a lot of money spent. The effect was oppressive.

'The dogs don't come in here,' said Mrs Marriner.

Pippa thought she had better not go in there, unless she took her shoes off first.

The money spent on that bedroom had not been spent downstairs, and Pippa knew enough to know what a good thing that was. No professional designer had been near the place — there was no trace of the fanciful hand of anybody like Pippa's late boss. Pippa recognized the look of the place, from other country houses that she knew: rooms had been done up over the years as they needed it — when damp patches could no longer be ignored, or peeling paper, or falling plaster. Insofar as any taste was shown, it was deeply conservative. The colours were muted. Some of the curtains and chair covers were beginning to be threadbare, and some of the rugs were reaching the end of their useful lives. The effect was comforting. It was obvious that Mrs Marriner had had nothing to do with any of it — she had bought or inherited the whole lot as it stood. She had spent money on one room only — imposed her personality on that room only.

She did not like her horses or dogs or hens or doves. She did not seem to like her house either.

'It's all as my great-aunt left it,' said Mrs Marriner.

It was not obvious whether this was a boast or an apology. Was the comfortable, shabby old house being preserved as a kind of shrine to the great-aunt, in a kind of piety? Was Mrs Marriner talking as might the owner of a Palladian villa?

The furniture was Georgian and Victorian, decent, not very valuable. The pictures were Victorian. Some were of dogs and horses, and some were landscapes. They might have been acquired with love, but they would be sold by the yard.

All over the house there were books, thousands of big dark books. There were no frivolous modern books, no garish jackets, no paperbacks. People in the house might have read books in the last fifty years, but nobody here had bought one.

Pippa did not stop to look at the titles of the books. Even without stopping, she could see that they were very dusty.

Mrs Marriner saw that Pippa saw the dust. She said, 'There's supposed to be a Mrs Carter three mornings a week, but she broke a toe falling off her bicycle.'

'I'll try to get round as much as I can.'

'Yes.'

There was a breakfast room or utility room next to the kitchen, with a brick floor and pine furniture, the kind of room which made sense if you had servants or children or a messy hobby such as pottery. It had a glass door opening on to a porch with a tiled roof, an eccentric Victorian addition to that side of the house. The porch was enclosed by fine wire netting, outside which were removable panels of clear polythene. This was the aviary. The middle and upper levels were occupied by two dozen busy canaries, most a very pale daffodil yellow, and the floor by a pair of small clockwork toys which, on examination, turned out to be Japanese quails.

'They're supposed to have fresh water once a day,' said Mrs Marriner. 'And you top up the seed in those green things.'

'Don't they have lettuce?' said Pippa. 'And chickweed and groundsel and stuff?'

'If you can be bothered,' said Mrs Marriner.

She was not interested in the aviary, or its adorable occupants. Why did she keep the birds? The canaries could be sold for five, eight, ten pounds each. Had she inherited the aviary with the house? Was there a clause of the will that required her to be custodian of the canaries?

Mrs Marriner would leave a typed list of necessary telephone numbers. She would leave feeding instructions for the horses, dogs and birds. She would leave instructions about clocks and fuses and indoor plants.

'Will I be able to get hold of you?' asked Pippa.

'No.'

'You're going to Rome?'

'I may be there. You understand that my flight's not booked yet. I'm waiting for a message. It'll be four or five days, possibly a week.'

This was highly unsatisfactory. It was arrogant and thoughtless. But it seemed that Pippa had the job, if she wanted it. She decided she did. She liked the house and the animals. Although she was not used to solitude, she did not think she would be lonely. She would be living free and getting twelve pounds a day clear, in cash, sixty in advance. She would breathe a lot of fresh air, take healthy exercise, go to bed early, and read a lot of serious books she had never got round to.

She would not think of Fenton Lowell, not once, all the time that she was there.

CHAPTER 3

'I must leave unexpectedly very early tomorrow morning. A man from the local garage is taking me to Heathrow. You must get here by midday. I'll leave the key with the newsagent in the village. That's Medwell Zelston. You came through it. He knows you're coming, and I've told him what you look like.'

Pippa wondered for a second how Mrs Marriner described her to a country newsagent. She made herself listen to the brisk, indifferent voice on the telephone.

'I've left fifty pounds in an envelope on the kitchen table. My car is being serviced while I'm away, so you will use yours. Everything you need to know is on a pad by the telephone in the hall. There is food for you for two or three days, and a week's food for the birds and dogs.'

There was no trace in Mrs Marriner's voice of 'I hope that's all right,' or 'Sorry for the short notice.'

Mrs Marriner said, 'I rely on you to be there by noon. The dogs will have been in all morning.'

Pippa began to talk about 'weather permitting', but before she had finished her sentence, Mrs Marriner had rung off.

Well, she was just off abroad. She had to pack. She was in a hurry.

'I knew who you was,' said the woman behind the counter in the little cluttered newsagent's shop, 'almost before you got out o' the car. That's the young lady come to look after Mrs Marriner's, says I to meself, an' me only problem now is to find the key she left wi' us.'

She was a thin woman of fifty, with pink lipstick which seemed to belong to another world. On her head was a mat of orange fibres, in texture resembling coconut matting, which was either a wig or hair treated to resemble a wig. She was friendly.

'Here's Mr Lewis, lord of all he surveys. He'll find that key.'

Mr Lewis was stooped and miserable. Diagonally over his scalp were glued a few strands of what was undoubtedly hair.

Mr Lewis found the key, a Yale tied with a bit of string to a brown cardboard tag.

'All things come to them as waits.'

'Go careful on them bends,' said Mr Lewis. 'There's lads wi' Fords.'

Pippa drove out of the hamlet of Medwell Zelston. She was careful on the bends, on the slow, hazardous side-road up the valley to the house.

The house looked empty and forlorn, although Mrs Marriner's part of it had only been empty for five hours. The horses were out in the paddock. When she got out of the car, Pippa heard the cluck of a bantam from somewhere aloft. There was a scattering of white doves on the eyebrows of the barn.

The house was the same, but different. A slate-grey sky gave it an unfamiliar face, took away its innocence, darkened the windows, made it secretive. It was bigger and quieter, and more specifically somebody else's.

The dogs would give her a welcome.

They didn't, really.

They had all probably heard the car, certainly the key in the lock. They were waiting for her, but it was not her they were waiting for. Mr Tomkins, the King Charles puppy, wriggled towards her, tail waving, but he backed away from her hand.

Bunbury, the old springer, sat in a basket in a corner of the hall. Jacob, the dachshund, barked, neither welcoming nor hostile but as though to show that he could. He made a lot of noise for such a small dog.

Pippa had a headache from driving in a bad light on the motorway. She said, 'Oh, shut up!' more fiercely than she meant. Jacob barked louder and more rapidly.

Pippa expected there to be a note on the hall table, a word of friendliness, apology, farewell. There was only a list of telephone numbers. Pippa could not imagine anybody not leaving a note under these circumstances. Mrs Marriner thought it was enough that she was leaving the dogs.

The dogs would need a run, after five hours. That was absolutely the first thing. Okay, dogs, come on out. First they wouldn't go out, then they wouldn't come in. Did it matter when she fed the bantams, the birds in the aviary? Probably it was written down somewhere; if not, the bantams would tell her.

It was getting towards time for Pippa's own lunch. What a bore, what a hassle, unless something was ready on the kitchen table; and Mrs Marriner had left in such a hurry there was nothing left ready on the table. Pippa's headache had taken away her hunger. She would have tea later, then a big supper. That, all on one's own, seemed a bore and a hassle too.

She had a big cup of instant coffee and a couple of paracetamol tablets. Though it was only just after lunch (the lunch she could not be bothered to have), the sky was darkening to a dirty slate. She unpacked the small number of possessions she had brought, into the shelves and drawers of the antiseptic bedroom she had been shown. Mr Tomkins came with her, and took socks and slippers under the bed.

Early as it was, the afternoon was by now too far advanced to embark on a walk with the dogs. It was time to deal with the horses. The dogs could run about. Would Jacob snap at the horses' heels? It seemed likely. She did not want a horse bolting away, or the dachshund brained by a kick.

She went out of the back door, and rounded the corner of the house on the way to the stables. To her amazement, there was a gleam of orange light through the window of the tack-room, and oblongs of fainter gold which were the windows of the looseboxes.

Had the light been on? Had Mrs Marriner left it on, putting the horses out in the dawn?

The tack-room was kept locked, the key hung on a small nail in a secret place. People burgled stables. There was a profitable trade in second-hand saddles.

Pippa went softly to the tool-shed. She unlocked it and groped in the semi-darkness for a hammer. She was angry. They thought she was a helpless girl, somebody they could ignore. They must think that — her car was parked in full view, and some of the windows of the house were lit. This robbery was bare-faced, a damned impertinence. Pippa thought herself into enough rage to give her courage to march up to the tack-room door. She had to be quick — this flash of angry courage would not last long.

Hunger, coffee and paracetamol had perhaps made her lightheaded. She was cross at the way she thought Mrs Marriner had treated her — hanging up the telephone when there were still questions to ask, leaving no note, no food, no apology and no welcome. It was a lousy way to behave. Pippa was more than ready to take it out on the robber.

She threw open the tack-room door, at the same time raising the hammer.

'What the hell...?' she began, in a voice of brassy aggression.

A man was leaning over the corn-bin, scooping a measure of oats into a bucket. He was dressed as a gnome, but in a tweed cap. He looked up from his bucket at Pippa standing in the door like an avenging fury. He put down the scoop and tugged off his cap, revealing an untidy thatch of mousey-brown hair. He was only a little man, not more than a couple of inches taller than Pippa. He was quite a young man, ten years older than herself. His clothes were ancient and shapeless, their original colours unguessable. His face was weather-beaten to a nut-brown colour; his eyes were a startling blue.

'A-ben ponderen,' he said slowly. 'A-do b'lieve 'at ol' Cavendish d'need a sight more nuts an' less o' they oats.'

'Cavendish,' repeated Pippa stupidly.

'At gurt ol' chesty-nut gelden.'

'Oh. The big horse. Yes.'

Pippa lowered the hammer slowly. It seemed there was no immediate need of hammers. But she was still alert and suspicious, like Jacob the dachshund.

It was not possible that anybody should speak as this small brown man was speaking. His voice was as sweet and leisurely as treacle; his accent was from an antique world, the speech of an Arcadian peasantry in some fanciful green forest.

If she understood him aright — and she was not at all sure she did — he was getting the feeds for the horses. He knew the horses. He was editing the instructions that Mrs Marriner had left. He thought he knew better. He was presumptuous. He was not exactly cocky in manner, but he was making an annoying assumption of superior knowledge.

'How did you get in here?' asked Pippa.

'A-ben usen 'at door a mort o' yearn.'

Mort, thought Pippa. *A mort o' yearn. Nobody talks like that —
nobody has done for a hundred and fifty years. Why is he putting on this
yokel act? Is it supposed to be endearing? Am I supposed to be put off my
guard?*

Irritation and the cold air were bringing Pippa's headache
back.

'It's getting dark,' she said. 'I must get the horses in.'

'Leave un to oi.'

'No.'

'So be,' he said placidly. He emptied the bucket into the
manger in one of the looseboxes, and took the halter-ropes off
a hook. He opened the tack-room door; he stood back with
something like a bow, for Pippa to precede him through the
door.

Fenton had done that — opened doors for her, stood back,
almost bowed. Not many Englishmen nowadays behaved like
that. Was this strange little yokel trying to be gallant? Pippa was
upset at being reminded of Fenton. She went crossly out.

The dogs were waiting for them in the yard. Mr Tomkins
hurled himself at the newcomer. This meant nothing. Old
Bunbury shook himself out of his apathy and showed
something like enthusiasm. Jacob did not bark or snap or
growl or offer to bite. He lost his credibility as an enemy of the
world. He was almost undignified, jabbing his long nose
peaceably at the stranger's shin.

The horses came in, to feeds ready in the mangers and hay
ready in the racks. The little man patted the quarters and pulled
the ears of each, as they stirred around in their feeds with their
muzzles. He seemed very much at home, too much at home,
taking too much for granted. Pippa regarded herself as having
been left in charge. It was her responsibility that the horses had
the right feeds and the dogs remembered their training.

'Thank you. I'll lock up now,' she said in a tone which was meant to be dignified but was, perhaps, a little hectoring.

'Ar, they'm suppen cheerful,' he said.

Out in the yard, he pulled a bicycle from a shadow. It was almost full dark now, but in a gleam of light from the house Pippa saw that it was a ramshackle elderly machine, looking as though assembled from bits of several bicycles.

'A bid ye a sweet night,' he said to Pippa. Astride the bicycle he said to the dogs, 'Comforten dreams, lads.' He wobbled away down the drive, without lights, the chain on the bicycle ticking in the cogs.

'Who are you?' Pippa suddenly called after him, a question she realized she might have asked some time before.

'A-ben Dan Mallett,' he called back.

He was already invisible in the darkness under the trees at the bottom of the drive.

The name rang a bell in Pippa's mind, clear and sinister. Dan Mallett the thief, the man not to allow into the house, the one who lived in a hovel with a senile hag.

They had let him out of prison, then.

Pippa had not expected somebody so small or so young — not much taller than herself, not so very much older. She had not expected such startling blue eyes.

Looking back on the previous half-hour, Pippa was puzzled at herself. She had really been rather brave, marching into the tack-room armed with a hammer, to confront what might have been a gang of marauders. She had been brave because she was angry. And then she had somehow persuaded herself, or been persuaded, to drop the hammer and the righteous anger and everything else, and tamely accept a lot of impertinence about the horses getting the wrong food. Bang, just like that. It wasn't as though she had liked him on sight, or trusted him, or been beguiled by his big blue eyes. (Did he have blue eyes? Perhaps they were blue. Perhaps they were quite big.) After Pippa's recent experience in London, she was not going to be beguiled so easily. She was certainly not about to be suckered by a small yokel in large trousers.

He did not look like a jailbird. Billy the Kid and Crippen did not look like murderers.

That treacly rural voice of his was just silly. It was practically impossible to understand. A voice you couldn't understand was counterproductive.

Had he put the horses out in the morning?

Was he going to be constantly about the place, intruding on Pippa's privacy and grief, officiously busying himself with the animals, irritating her with his cozening manner and his stupid voice?

'Don't let him into the house. If you do, count the spoons when he leaves.'

He was just out of prison. Probably he would soon be back in prison again, but for the moment he was an irritant and a pest and a threat.

Pippa had the renewed feeling, stronger than ever, that she should never have taken this job.

At seven o'clock, the telephone rang. Pippa was in the kitchen. The nearest extension was in the small sitting-room, just along the passage towards the hall. The telephone was on a writing-desk in the corner of the room, by a window. The desk had been put there, perhaps, after the socket had been installed for the telephone, because the flex came out from behind the desk.

There was an armchair beside the desk, which looked as though it had been put there for telephoning. It was almost impossible not to sit in that chair while talking on that instrument. Pippa found herself descending into the chair even as she reached for the telephone. It was a deep chair. Pippa understood that it would be conducive to long conversations.

Pippa did not intend a long conversation now. The call would not be for her. Nobody knew where she was.

She said, 'Hallo?'

'Judith?' said a man's voice.

'Mrs Marriner is not here.'

'Has she gone to Rome again?'

'I believe so.'

'For how long?'

'She wasn't sure. A few days. I can give her a message when she comes back.'

'Oh, I don't think I'll leave a message. She doesn't want a message from me.' There was something curious about the voice. It was as though he were speaking through a layer of fabric. There was something alarming about it. It was a false voice, as though somebody were imitating somebody else.

'Who is that speaking, please?' said Pippa.

'A mystery man,' he said. 'A shadow on the ceiling. I dance and prance like a will-o'-the-wisp, and nobody catches me...' His voice took on a kind of archness, a joke-making tone. It sounded boastful. It even sounded slightly idiotic. He said, 'I'll call again, in case you have news of your hostess.'

Pippa began to say that she did not expect any news, but the caller rang off.

It would all seem saner in the morning. The morning was a long way off. This was only the first evening. Of how many evenings? Ten? Twenty? That had been left in the air, since Pippa had no commitments of any kind, not without a job or a flat or Fenton Lowell. The job had seemed to depend on being open-ended. That was ridiculous. She should never have consented to such an arrangement. Only misery and purposelessness and a screaming need to get out of London had induced her to land in this trap.

The place was full of little insinuating men in baggy trousers, and there were calls on the telephone from men with unpleasant voices.

Apathetically, Pippa contemplated the need for dinner. She discovered that she was ravenous. It was hardly surprising. Her headache had gone, although she might have expected it to return. She decided on a defiant fry-up, extravagant and unhealthy, a meal that would make a merry noise in the pan. In the kitchen she found a pan, lard, bacon, eggs, bread, unseasonable tomatoes. It was a meal out of childhood, a meal she could never have given Fenton. Cooking such a meal for herself was a gesture of defiant independence. The monstrous spluttering of frying tomatoes was a hymn of courage sung cheerfully in the face of impertinent little men and sinister telephone voices — it was a crackle of magic to exorcise the spirit of Fenton Lowell.

The dogs settled themselves in the places where they settled. Bunbury heaved about, getting comfortable under the kitchen table, Jacob slithered miraculously upwards into his chair, Mr Tomkins climbed into his bean-bag and then climbed out again. He begged shamelessly at Pippa's knee. Conscientiously she restrained herself from giving him any scraps.

The telephone rang. Pippa had a notion to let it ring. In London, in certain moods, she might have done so. Here she had to answer it.

She swore, using a word of Fenton's imported from New York. She trotted into the small sitting-room, wondering why Mrs Marriner did not have an extension in the kitchen.

'Hallo?'

'I don't know your name,' said a quacking female voice, 'but I can just about see your lights over the valley. You can see mine, if you go to the top of the house and look south. Not this minute!' The caller barked with laughter, a noise like a machine gun. It was not really laughter. 'The name's Craik. I'm Mary Craik. Judith Marriner probably left our name and number with you. Feel free to use it if there's a crisis. Leave a message on the machine if we're out. I'll try and look in some time tomorrow. Moral support. Have some low-calorie tonic on ice.' She barked her mirthless laugh again.

Pippa had heard this voice before, at cocktail parties and in the hunting field, more often in the country than in London, more often in the Shires than in gentler, remoter places; this was a tough, rich, middle-aged woman who pretended not to watch television, despised the local hunt, was permanently cross not to have married a duke.

Pippa's supper was getting cold, congealing on her plate. She could not cut short a conversation which, however uncongenial, was presumably made out of kindness.

The call finished at last — her glass being empty, Pippa thought. Pippa went back to her supper. Her heart sank at the thought of a visit from the owner of that laugh.

Pippa had the curious certainty that the telephone would ring again. The dogs thought so too. They were alert. The kitchen was full of a sense of expectancy, like a theatre when the house-lights go down. The ringing of the telephone would have been a relief, though perhaps not the conversation that followed.

Pippa ate all that she could be bothered with. She scraped away the rest, and put the greasy plate in the washing-up bowl to soak. It was not the right sort of dinner to have had; she wished she had cooked something quite different. The telephone remained silent. She patrolled the house, every room of Mrs Marriner's part of the house, with the feeling that this was her duty as custodian. She wondered again why a woman living alone should want such a large establishment. The lights were bright, the shadows were dark. She tried to bring the dogs with her on her tour of inspection, but they hung back, lazy or waiting for something.

Pippa went out and across the yard to make sure the horses were all right. They might want hay or water. The scruffy little man might not have given them enough. It was in any case something to do for a bit. The time was still only ten o'clock.

The dogs were not interested in coming out with her. It was not yet their time for their final run. Pippa was careful not to lock herself out. The outside light washed over the flagstones of the back yard, and the light from the windows over the gravel beside the house.

The horses were sleepy. One of them was lying down in its box, straw in its mane and tail. They had hay and water enough for the night and the early morning.

There was a muted conversation among the bantams in the hayloft, disturbed by the light in the stable below.

Everything was all right, and another five minutes had crawled by. Going back towards the house, Pippa heard the sharp yap of the dachshund. The other dogs began to bark, even old Bunbury, their voices excited, urgent. Why? The telephone had not rung. Jacob had started the others barking, but what had started him? The night was still, absolutely quiet. There was no sound of traffic from the road. There was no sign of anything outside the house. Inside, the dogs were barking and running about.

Pippa wanted Fenton Lowell. She wanted anybody.

She wanted to get her mother's car and drive a long way from this place. Mr Tomkins wriggled up to her as she went in by the back door. His nose against her knee reminded her that running away was absolutely not one of the options.

Anyway, she had nowhere to go.

There was a burglar alarm on the wall over the front door. Mrs Marriner had said nothing about it, and Pippa had not thought to ask. It was not mentioned in her listed instructions. Pippa had never set a burglar alarm, and had no idea how to do so. There might be a way she could find out how to set this one in the morning; there was no way she could find out that night. Even if not working, it might have a deterrent effect. Pippa knew people who had dummy burglar alarms, to frighten criminals away. That would only work if the alarm was seen; that meant leaving the outside light on all night; that gave the impression that whoever was living in the house had gone out.

It was still only ten thirty. It was too early for bed, too early for the dogs' last run. If she went to bed, she would not sleep. There was still plenty of evening for something to happen in. The dogs thought something was going to happen.

With Fenton, Pippa had got quite out of the way of watching television. But this seemed a time for it. This seemed the moment for which television was invented.

None of the channels had anything she could bring herself to care about. The people were all making too much noise. Even without the sound, you could tell they were shouting, or banging guitars, or being laughed at by a studio audience.

Pippa thought of Fenton's contempt, that she should be sitting staring at a screen for lack of anything better to do; she basked for a moment in the thought of his approval when she switched it off.

The dogs went out and came in. They went each to his usual bed, revolved, snuffled, lay curled. Pippa envied their innocent confidence, aware that the thought was familiar and unhelpful. Two weeks before she had faced life as they did, certain of goodwill, a sweet sleep, the next meal.

Pippa checked bolts, locks, window catches. She turned off the downstairs lights. She filled a hot-water bottle from the electric kettle in her bedroom, the antiseptic guest-room which did not yet feel like home. When she was ready for bed, she opened the big sash window a little at the top; she opened the curtains so that daylight would wake her. She slid between clean, cold sheets. She found that she was exhausted but wakeful. She tried and failed to make any sense of the day.

Unanswered questions circled in her mind like fish in a bowl. Fears poked up their heads over the sill of awareness, and trailed dark wings in upper corners.

It was being tired, being in a strange bed, being offered so many puzzles.

In the morning, answers would be found. She would go and look for them. It was simply a matter of asking questions. Now the night was completely black, the oblong of the window invisible, an unfamiliar situation, something impossible in London. When the window was full of light and filled the room with light, things would wear a different aspect.

She heard footsteps on the gravel outside her window.

Her first surprising reaction was one of pure rage. *I'm tired, I've had enough today, why the bloody hell can't they leave me alone?*

She thought — *I wasn't warned about this. I wasn't prepared, I wasn't briefed, I wasn't warned to expect people prowling round the house in the middle of the night. The damned Marriner woman swans off irresponsibly to Italy, leaving me all alone here with things I can't cope with.*

She thought — *I thought I was tough and adult, but I'm too young for this. I don't know enough. I'm not tough enough.*

She got out of bed and groped to the window. It was the first thing to do. Going downstairs might come later.

Jacob began to bark. All three dogs barked. Pippa had not imagined the footsteps. The dogs had heard them. Surely nobody would break in, hearing the barking of all those dogs?

Pippa decided to fill the house with light, to give the impression that it was full of people, that an army had arrived during the evening. She ran about, turning on switches. It was half-past midnight. She let the dogs out of the kitchen but not out of the house. They barked intermittently, uneasily. Pippa's alarm infected them; their alarm infected Pippa. There was something hysterical about the four of them running about.

Pippa shouted, 'John! Henry! Freddy! Have you got the shotgun?'

She felt foolish, but it seemed a good idea.

The dogs were puzzled, taking the shouts to be for them, not knowing why their names had been changed.

Nothing else happened, nothing at all.

The dogs at last went back to sleep. Pippa badly wanted to do the same, but tension had made her hopelessly wakeful. She made herself a cup of Ovaltine, doing everything carefully, not allowing her hands to shake, not allowing the milk to boil over.

The house was cold, the timer having switched off the central heating three hours before.

She sat drinking her Ovaltine in the kitchen, Bunbury snoring softly across her feet. His snores were so reassuring that Pippa did not want to leave them. She could not sit up all night. There was plenty to do in the morning.

The lights? A small Puritan voice told her to turn them all off. Another voice said to leave them all on. She compromised. She turned them all off, except those in the hall and on the stairs.

Anybody who came to do anything would have done it by now, and gone away.

Pippa went to bed in her clean cold room, wishing she were doing so in almost any other room in the world.

CHAPTER 4

The wind went round in the night, and the morning was warm and blustery, a day more like March than January. Everything did look better. Probably there had been no footstep crunching the gravel in the night.

Pippa let the dogs out as soon as she was downstairs. Old Bunbury had to be prodded awake, and then prodded to go out. Pippa pulled a coat on over her dressing-gown and went out with them. Of course there was nothing to be seen. There was no Man Friday footprint. The horses were all right, the tack-room locked, her car not stolen.

Pippa put the kettle on and then consulted her instructions.

She gave Mr Tomkins his breakfast, since he was still on two meals a day. She kept the others out of the kitchen while he was eating it, and gave them a couple of biscuits each.

In the aviary, two or three of the canaries were making tentative experiments in singing, trilling and peeping softly as though tuning up for the major effort of the spring. The cock of the pair of quails, busy in the sawdust on the floor, was making a kind of small shout, as though bidding the world good morning, and telling Pippa to hurry up with his breakfast. She topped up the hoppers with seed for the canaries, dumped a handful of chick-crumbs on the floor for the quail, and changed the water. Immediately the pot of clean water was back, one of the canaries had a vigorous bath, splashing so much water about that the pot was nearly empty. Pippa filled it again. She wondered how many times a day she would find herself doing that; she wondered how many times Mrs Marriner did it.

The house was now full of light, with an occasional gleam of sun offered and snatched away by the hurrying clouds.

Finishing her coffee after breakfast, Pippa tried to make a mental list of things to do. Wash up and tidy the kitchen. Make her bed. Put the horses out. Then what? No shopping needed to be done; if she went to the village, it would be for the sake of doing so. Garage? She had filled up the car on the way down. Hoovering? Dusting? Maybe a bit of that, later. Walking the dogs? Definitely for later, for after lunch, if she could be bothered with lunch.

Whatever items she added to this list, it was a pretty dim programme. Was she really a country girl?

All three dogs had gone back to bed, back to sleep, as though exhausted by the effort of waking up. Pippa knew how they felt.

Pippa crossed the yard on her way to put the horses out and saw with astonishment that they were already out. Cavendish, the big chestnut gelding, was wearing a New Zealand rug. Probably that was right, because he was trace-clipped. The others were unclipped; they had good heavy woolly coats; in this warm breeze they were doubtless more comfortable as they were. Whoever put them out had decided so, anyway. Who? The little criminal with the treacly voice and the strange archaic language? Was he *meant* to come and deal with the horses? Was he paid to? Mrs Marriner had said something about him coming to do the garden. She said he would want the money, when he got out of prison. Was Pippa supposed to pay him? There was nothing about that in the typewritten instructions.

There was no sign of the little man, or of any other man: just the horses placidly grazing in the nearest of the paddocks.

Pippa stood irresolute in the middle of the yard. Her mind listed not the things she had to do but the questions she wanted answered. About all these unloved animals and birds, and the late Mr Marriner, and nine rooms occupied by one widow, and little sinister criminals in baggy trousers...

But how could she ask these questions, and who could she ask them of? The orange-haired woman in the newsagent's? The frightening Mrs Craik across the valley?

Did Mrs Marriner have a boyfriend in Rome?

On balance, Pippa felt annoyed that the horses had been dealt with. She felt deflated. She had come out of the house full of purpose, a task ahead of her. She liked physical contact with horses, patting them, leading them. She liked their size and soft-heartedness, their strength and dependence. She liked the way they felt and smelled.

She had liked the prospect of a task which could be stretched to take half an hour.

At least there was the mucking out to do. She collected the pitchfork and trundled the wheelbarrow into the stables.

The boxes were perfectly clean, with fresh bedding on the floor. The buckets had been filled too.

All this had been done while she was having breakfast. Very quickly, but also very quietly. How had he persuaded the horses to cross the yard on tiptoe?

Was he going to come every day, twice a day, putting the horses out and bringing them in, mucking out and feeding, and probably grooming and picking out their feet?

It gave Pippa altogether too much time for housework. She recoiled at the thought of taking out and dusting all those books, but with the horses taken care of, her conscience would probably oblige her to do that kind of thing. Blast the interfering little man with his syrupy voice and his air of knowing best and his secret comings and goings.

Probably she should feel gratitude, but she was not in a mood for gratitude.

Even in the benevolent light of the morning, she was in a mood to be jumpy and suspicious.

There was something stealthy about his creeping in and doing the horses behind her back. There was something deceitful about it.

Pippa was sure nothing had been said about any such arrangement. If Mrs Marriner had expected it to happen, she would have said so. She had not expected it. It was not part of her plan at all. It was his plan. He had a reason for doing the horses. It was an excuse for coming here, for creeping about in the paddock and the yard and the stables.

Perhaps he was going to be creeping about in the house. Perhaps he had already been doing so.

It was his footstep on the gravel in the middle of the night. Furtive as he was, he could not help a small crunching noise when he put his foot down on gravel. Pippa had heard it because she was wide awake in a silent, sleeping world.

She strolled indecisively out onto the lawn. It was covered with thousands of worm-casts, which were strewn over the damp moss as though scattered there by a gigantic pepper-mill. In the rough grass beyond the lawn, under small ornamental trees, there was a rash of brand new molehills. It would be terrible if their workings advanced into the lawn. It seemed highly likely. Was there anything she could do about that? There was a metal object in the tool-shed that might be a mole-trap, but Pippa had no idea how or where to set it. She had heard that you baited the runs with worms doctored with strychnine. That seemed a disgusting thing to do, dangerous for the dogs and for birds. In any case, it was probably difficult to get hold of strychnine. Pippa looked at the worm-casts and mole-hills in dismay.

Some of the things she was here to do were done already by somebody else, and some she was incapable of.

She was terrified out of her wits in the middle of the night.

The new courage and cheerfulness of the morning had evaporated. She was less and less complacent by the minute. She felt inadequate.

Over the anonymous clumps and stumps in the border at the side of the lawn, there were squadrons of busy flies. They had either hatched or woken up in the unseasonable warmth of the air. There seemed to be no purpose in their circlings. There were bees about as well, unhurried brown ladies showing a mild interest in the lovely pink-white paperweights of the viburnum blossom. Flies by day, moths by night, had alerted armies of spiders. As Pippa watched, there were two — one large, one small — spanning with webs the corners of the pergola, flinging themselves out into space, unreeling as they flew invisible silk lines. And on a fence-post in a windless corner a tortoiseshell butterfly moved its wings with tentative gestures, as though making sure that they worked.

Further down in the rough grass, at the very top of a silver birch, a song-thrush celebrated the warm air, or defied trespassers on his pitch, or announced his desire for a wife. In the lower branches of another tree a robin was singing. *Ti-choo* said a great tit, showing off his gymnastics among the twigs. Out of the tangle of big trees beyond burst a green woodpecker, laughing like an idiot.

Horses, dogs, insects, birds — the place was thronged with company, but Pippa was lonely. To her disgust, she wanted somebody to talk to. She had supposed that licking wounds was best done in solitude, but all that solitude was giving her was the hump. It was no good spotting all these miracles of nature without somebody to point them out to.

Not little men in baggy trousers, but somebody like Fent... No!

'We did imagine she'd sell,' said the woman in the newsagent's shop. 'Didn't we, Mr Lewis? "She'll sell," we said, with one voice. The moment her auntie died, leaving it lock, stock and barrel. Also livestock, which you, dear, know about better than most. Old Mrs Hodges was a lady with a will of iron. "She wields a rod of iron," I used to say, didn't I, Mr Lewis? Well, take it from me that I did, though his lordship may not have been listenin' even then. The iron fist, she had, an' not much velvet glove with it neither.'

The woman scratched her scalp through the coconut matting which covered it, with the point of a pair of scissors.

'Stop doin' that, do,' said Mr Lewis miserably. 'What d'ye think you are, an ol' sow wi' a barbed wire fence?'

'Always one for the gracious phrase,' said the woman comfortably to Pippa. 'Such a pleasure to be associated with.'

The shop was very small, the walls stacked from floor to ceiling with a strange variety of merchandise — food, toothpaste, plastic sandals, children's colouring books, watering cans. It smelled of detergent and tobacco, though these aromas might have come from the people rather than the goods. None of the things which Pippa wanted were to be had in that shop, except information.

Colonel and Mrs Hodges had bought Parsonage Farm back in BC some time — that is to say, soon after the war. The Colonel managed to bring an old soldier with him, as a sort of all-purpose manservant, and they also had a woman, described as a busy old bundle, who had been the Hodges' children's nurse. By local standards, the Hodges thus lived plutocratically. The Colonel went shooting in the autumn, fox-hunting in the winter and fishing in the summer. He was also Chairman of the Parochial Church Council and so forth and so forth, and Mrs Hodges was Chairman of the Flower show and President of the Women's Institute and so forth.

The children had grown up and gone away, and died or were disinherited or something (vagueness shrouded parts of the history), but still the old Hodges wanted all of that big house, and all the dogs and horses.

And then, as though to give a point to it all, Miss Judith came into their lives. Of course, she had been there all along, but she started coming to Medwell. Judith Duxbury she was then, a great-niece to be exact, quite the little lady even as a tiny, kept herself ever so clean and tidy, never one for sploshing in the mud or running wild.

When the Colonel died, Mrs Hodges might have sold up and gone away. But she had a new reason for keeping it all. She had Miss Judith. What the old lady did do was split the house in two, and let half of it. She kept the bigger half for Miss Judith to live in, and a stable full of horses for Miss Judith to ride, and Miss Judith grew up, and got herself engaged to be married, two or three times, and none of what Pippa was being told was a breach of confidence. How could it be, because everybody knew it?

The years went by, and it began to look as though Miss Judith left it a bit late, no plain gold band in spite of all those gentlemen. But she made it in the end: Mr Jack, a bit younger than herself. A small London wedding they had, which was disappointing for folk in the village. Miss Judith — Mrs Marriner as now was — still came to Medwell quite often. Mr

Jack never came in the summer, because what he liked was his sailing. Never happy except when afloat on the briny, with a yo ho and so forth, but there's no accounting for tastes. Miss Judith freely said she couldn't abide the sea — said it repeatedly, to anybody who'd listen.

Then there was the two deaths almost simultaneously, a dreadful shock to all. Mrs Hodges keeled over while in the very act of arranging tulips in a vase — it all went for six — flowers, water, bits of broken china. And Jack Marriner was lost at sea. Not very far out to sea, neither. It was only a little boat he was in. They found the boat, but they never found him.

'They mounted a hernormous search,' said Mr Lewis glumly, 'wi' taxpayers' money.'

'And never found hair nor hide,' said the woman, renewing the scratching of her own hide through her own hair.

This answered some of the questions about which Pippa had been curious — how Mrs Marriner came to own such a big place and so many animals. But it did not answer the question of why she still owned these things. To inherit three horses, yes. But for her, uninterested, to keep them? To keep all those echoing empty chilly dusty rooms, all those acres of valuable paddocks?

It was as much of a surprise to the village as it was to Pippa.

'We all jus' jumped to the conclusion she'd put the 'ole boiling on the market.'

'Very well put, Mr Lewis. Wasn't that neatly put?'

'Perhaps she couldn't,' suggested Pippa. 'Perhaps there was something in the will.'

'Miss Judith,' said the woman, 'Mrs Marriner as now is, wouldn't be given pause by no consideration of that order. If she wanted to sell, she'd find a way to do it. There's lawyers can twiddle a will around so once you got your hands on you can do as you please.'

Pippa thought this was probably true.

She bought a ball of string, feeling obliged to justify her presence in the shop for so long. It was the least useless to her of all the objects she could see.

On her way out, she said, 'By the way, do you know a man called Dan Mallett?'

'Ow!' said Mr Lewis, as though in pain. 'There's a villain. Keep your pockets buttoned up when he's by. Ow! You don't want nothing to do wi' Dan Mallett.'

'I don't know so much,' said the woman. 'I don't know so much.'

'There you go, standin' up for him, like all 'alf-witted females,' said Mr Lewis.

'I speak as I feel,' said the woman. 'Incapable o' deception.'

'All the young girls goes gooey about that bloke,' said Mr Lewis to Pippa. 'All the old cows does likewise.'

'I b'lieve he has reference to persons here present,' said the woman. 'But too tactful to name names. Diplomatic as always, it's an education an' a privilege to listen.'

'Why do all the girls go gooey about him?' asked Pippa, laughing but also uneasy.

'He weaves a spell,' said the woman. 'You'll see.'

'He gets away wi' murder,' said Mr Lewis.

'Breaks all the commandments, he does,' said the woman, 'every hour on the hour.'

A woman got out of a Volvo on the gravel beside the house. She was wearing a mid-length Barbour and a tweed deerstalker. She had thin lips in a face with otherwise large features. She might have been forty, or rather more: cold weather was not kind to her complexion. Pippa instantly identified her as the caller of the previous evening, the neighbour over the valley.

Pippa had expected her, but not quite as soon.

'Just called round to make sure that everything's all right,' she said, in that yapping tone of command that made Pippa want to disobey. 'Judith Marriner does it for me, when I'm away. Which I practically never am.' She barked with meaningless, mirthless laughter. 'Practically never.'

Mary Craik went round behind the stables to the rail of the first paddock. She was checking up on the horses. But she scarcely glanced at them. She was going through the motions of checking up. Looking at the horses was an excuse for coming (as looking after the horses was an excuse for Dan Mallett coming). Mrs Craik was here for some reason that had nothing to do with horses.

Her thin lips were brilliantly red in the spongy whiteness of her face. Her eyebrows were very thin, as though abolished and then redrawn in a new place. The effect was formidable but very dated. It was as though Mrs Craik had fallen asleep in 1935, a female fox-hunting Rip Van Winkle, and only just woken up.

Pippa amused herself for a moment by imagining the effect of this woman on Fenton Lowell. He would stare at her in horrified fascination, and then try to get her talking about her attitude to sex and religion. The memory of Fenton was painful, but it was a pretty good antidote to Mrs Craik.

Being more or less polite to the neighbours was probably part of Pippa's duties. Certainly she should not antagonize anybody. So she said, 'Won't you come in for a minute?'

'I was proposing to, thank you very much,' said Mrs Craik, which Pippa thought as graceless a remark as she had ever heard.

She accepted a cup of instant coffee in the kitchen. She sat drinking it as though she were listening for something.

Even Mr Tomkins, friend of all the world, seemed less than crazy about Mrs Craik.

'Of course, it was a godsend to us,' she said, 'that the Marriners decided to live here. Most of the neighbours are so old they've retired from being retired.' She gave a burst of laughter, in appreciation of her epigram.

'I understand Mrs Marriner inherited the house,' said Pippa, since a reply seemed required of her.

'Might have sold, though. Jack Marriner wasn't really what I call a country-man. Of course, I myself come from Leicestershire.'

'Oh yes.'

'Where things are a little different. This place is what I call Sleepy Hollow.'

'Oh yes.'

'Most of the people are so old they've retired from their retirement.' She laughed again, as though the joke was even funnier the second time round.

She stayed longer than anybody could have expected, far longer than Pippa wanted. It was as though she was herself killing time — as though she had nothing to do, no house or animals of her own.

She was waiting for something. She was waiting for somebody to come, for a message to arrive.

Even though Judith Marriner was away? Or because Judith Marriner was away?

When at last she resumed her Barbour, and strode mannishly out to her Volvo, she was still looking round alertly. What for? What was there to be scrutinized that she had not already looked at? What was she waiting for? Who was she waiting for?

There was one person who might come at any moment — who had already come and would probably come again. Could that be it?

Pippa said, 'Can you tell me anything about a man called Dan Mallett?'

'Everybody for miles around can tell you all about that little bastard,' said Mrs Craik. 'People use him for odd jobs. My lamented mother-in-law used him. I wouldn't have him on the place. He pinches everything that isn't nailed down and most things that are.' The machine gun laugh finished this speech.

Whoever Mary Craik was waiting for, looking for, it wasn't Dan Mallett.

Pippa walked the dogs. Mr Tomkins was extremely anxious to come. Jacob only wanted to kill things. The day had become lovely, and the air and the wet warm ground were full of ridiculously early promise. There was a scattering of lambs among the ewes in a huge field that sloped down towards the river. Pippa put Mr Tomkins as well as Jacob on the lead. They were the first lambs Pippa had seen. They might be just about the first anybody had seen — lambing would be early in this soft south-western countryside. All the lambs Pippa could see, as it happened, had their backs towards her. She remembered a saying of the country people of her childhood, that if you saw the tails of the first lambs that you saw, something terrible was going to happen.

The air and the exercise and the misty, benevolent sun had pushed away Pippa's uneasiness, her certainty in the night that coming here had been a really bad idea. Should the frail, skinny behinds of new-born lambs revive all those fears of footsteps in the small hours?

Out on the shoulder of the hill above the river, with the dogs all round her like the minders round a pop-singer, Pippa felt happy and safe. But she had to turn, and to hurry through the lengthening shadows back to the house. Old Bunbury had walked far enough, and the horses had to be brought in and put to bed.

As she more than half expected, the horses did not have to be brought in. They did not have to be fed or watered.

It was nice, in a way. It would have been nice, if she had had other things to do.

The little man broke all the commandments. All the girls went gooey at the sight of him. You had to count the spoons, and keep your pockets buttoned up, and he pinched anything even if it was nailed down.

None of these things looked very likely when he pulled the ears of Talisman, the shaggy dun, and then said a gentle goodnight to Dorothy, the bay mare, who was very stiff in the joints.

None of the horses could be ridden, because none was shod. Dorothy was probably past it anyway. They were all pensioners, it seemed, left behind by the great-aunt. Pippa wondered why Cavendish, the chestnut, was clipped. Perhaps he was still ridden by somebody, though not, Pippa thought, by Mrs Marriner. Certainly there was tack enough for a regiment of lancers.

'Aren't they ever going to be shod?' she asked suddenly.

'Ay, some when.'

'Does anybody ride them?'

"At Cavendish, Massr Craik d'come wi' boot an' spur. D'come yere and be riden a score o' years.'

Mr Craik came over here from his family's home over the valley, its windows said to be in sight, though Pippa had not identified them. Mr Craik had been coming for a score of years, and meeting Mrs Marriner, all those years, long before she was Mrs Marriner.

Did this explain anything at all? Though they had both married other people?

'Don't the Craiks keep horses of their own?' she asked. She had been taught not to gossip with servants, but this leprechaun was not exactly a servant, and anyway, servants always had the best gossip.

'Up Berryes? A-baint space f' t'keep 'arsen.'

Pippa heard 'arson' and was baffled. After a moment, she understood that she was expected to believe in an antique plural of an antique pronunciation of 'horse'. She thought it only barely possible that a man who was still young — hardly ten years older than herself — could use such a word in the ordinary way, unless he was putting on the most ridiculous act.

His eyes were exceedingly blue. His expression was bashful. He was not to be trusted an inch.

The Craiks had no room to keep horses, though Mr Craik came here to ride regularly, and though Mrs Craik came from Leicestershire and looked it. Mrs Craik rode other and better horses, perhaps tall thoroughbreds from the Shires, property of a neighbouring duke? That was the way she looked and sounded.

If she did that, why did she come prying at these horses?

Pippa wanted more answers from this Dan Mallett creature, but she thought it would be undignified to ask the questions.

Meanwhile, the horses were done, and soon the dogs would be done, and then the evening stretched ahead.

Dan Mallett wobbled away on his bicycle through the gathering darkness. Pippa was left alone with the dogs, and with whatever was going to happen during all the long hours of the evening.

The telephone rang. Jacob barked at it. Pippa took it in the small sitting-room.

'Hallo?'

A voice said, '*Pronto.*' There were clicks and buzzes, and then a sense rather than a sound of background music and conversation.

'Hallo,' said a female voice. 'Is that Philippa Lees? Judith Marriner here. Is everything all right?'

'Yes, fine. Where are you? How was your flight?'

'All right. I can't linger to chat. I'm calling from a public box. I'm just ringing to make sure the house hasn't burned down.'

'No. Everything's fine, but while you're on I do want to ask…'

'Any messages? Anything important?'

'There was a man — I don't know — who was odd. He wouldn't leave a name.'

'Then I don't suppose it was important. Don't forget the bantams. Wind the long-case clock on Sunday — I don't think I wrote that down.'

'Can you give me a number? Can I call you back?'

'No. I'm just off. The car's waiting. I'll ring again in a day or two.'

'Are you in Rome?'

But the call ended. Either Judith Marriner had hung up, or her money had run out.

Presumably she didn't know when she'd be back, or it would have been the first thing she'd said. Wouldn't it? She had not shown herself outstandingly bothered about other people's feelings or convenience.

They were a tough lot in this part of the country. It was all a long way from Thomas Hardy.

Later, much later, Pippa had finished her supper. In spite of good resolutions, she had eaten it too quickly. Like most people eating alone, she either gobbled or, if reading, forgot the food and let it congeal and grow cold.

It was another reason — one among so very many — for hating being alone, for missing Fenton.

She scrutinized once again the innumerable spines of books. It was hard to believe there was no book here that was less than fifty years old. There were some books only a little older than that — books written between the wars by Galsworthy, Hugh Walpole, H.G. Wells — but most were fifty years older than that again. There were complete sets of forgotten Victorians, which Pippa guessed were unread even when new. There was nothing distracting enough to stop her from gobbling her supper. But what a strange household.

Shamefacedly she turned on the television. She turned it off again. She read a couple of chapters of a G. A. Henty story, written for young schoolboys, about the Crusades. At ten she went to look at the horses, leaving the dogs indoors. This was not her choice but theirs.

The horses ignored her. They were all right. She straightened the stable-rug over Cavendish's quarters.

She was still in the stable when Jacob began to bark like a madman. The others began to bark. There was no sign of anybody. There had been no other sound.

CHAPTER 5

The last time the dogs had barked for no reason, there had been a very good reason.

Nobody would break in with all that noise going on.

Pippa went confidently to the back door. It was shut, as she had left it. She thought the barking was coming from the kitchen. She went in, locking and bolting the door behind her. Mr Tomkins rushed to greet her or warn her.

Pippa thought she would make herself a hot drink, and then read another chapter of her schoolboy's adventure story. It was a soothing book, which would not give her bad dreams.

The kitchen door was ajar. It had swung back into that position after Mr Tomkins pushed through. As Pippa opened it, she was wondering if she could think of an excuse to telephone anybody.

There was a man sitting at the kitchen table.

Pippa stopped short. She made a small, silly noise, a sort of sketch at a scream. She found she had both hands over her mouth, like a bad actress registering terror.

He was a big man, tall, broad-shouldered, his hair sandy and thinning, his face with a high colour and a high polish — the face of a man, as Pippa recognized, who had a lot of exercise and a lot of alcohol. He was about forty-five. He was dressed roughly but not cheaply, in a heavy sweater and corduroys.

'Found the house deserted,' he said, his voice harsh but not unattractive. 'Bad idea. I take it you're the bird who's supposed to be looking after the place.'

Pippa was minded to tell the intruder to mind his own business, and to ask him how he dared to walk uninvited into a lady's house in the middle of the night. But when she opened her mouth, it came out differently. 'I only went as far as the stables,' she said defensively.

'Very proper. Have you heard from Mrs Marriner?'

'Yes, she said she was calling from — I mean, um, who are you?'

'Michael Craik.'

Pippa realized that she had already known this. She wondered if the Craiks behaved so cavalierly when Mrs Marriner was about.

Michael Craik was looking at her as, obviously, he looked at all pretty girls. He looked her up and down. It was an offensive, bullying sort of look. He almost licked his lips. He said, 'I undertook, in a neighbourly way, to keep an eye on things.'

'Oh,' said Pippa, 'Mrs Craik has been doing that, too.'

'Probably. She's grabbing the chance of a look round. She's not usually allowed in here.'

'Oh,' said Pippa. She waited for him to say some more, but he was not going to say any more. 'How did you get in?' she said.

'Through the door, you silly little thing, you having obligingly left it open.'

'I did not.'

'In the American sense, of unlocked.'

Well, that was right. Fenton had said 'open' to mean unlocked. 'But I didn't hear you,' said Pippa. 'I didn't hear a car.'

'No, you didn't. So Judy rang from Rome, did she? I hope she's having good weather. I was in Rome in January once — it was colder than Bognor on August Bank Holiday.' Michael

Craik laughed, his laugh not unlike his wife's, a mirthless noise made by a machine, a motorbike or outboard.

He stood up. He went to a kitchen cabinet, to one of a dozen identical white-painted doors. He opened it on to a couple of shelves of jars and bottles. He reached without hesitation for a jar of instant coffee.

'Don't you think?' he said. 'I won't ask you for whisky.'

He knew exactly where Mrs Marriner kept her instant coffee. Could it be true that his wife was not allowed in here? What was going on among these unpleasant people?

Michael Craik filled the electric kettle, plugged it in, switched it on. He had done these things a hundred times before. He was completely at home.

'It's a great thing to have a man about the house,' he said, 'to master the technology of modern living.' He barked with laughter again, his wife's laughter. He thought he had made a joke.

It was a big kitchen, but he overfilled it. He radiated a kind of raw energy. He was a bully. He was gentle with the dogs, though, affectionate and patient. In that high-coloured face, he had very pale grey eyes.

He got two mugs out of the cupboard, knowing where to go for them and for spoons and sugar. He said, 'I suppose it's too much to hope that Judy gave you a number?'

'She told me before she left she couldn't be reached. She called from a box. I think she was calling from a bar or something.'

'Ah. Very wise, really. If you're getting away, get away. Like poor little Jack. He, perhaps, overdid it.'

'Did Mr Marriner get caught in a sudden high wind, or what?'

'He got caught with his fingers in the till. This is a matter of universal local knowledge, so I am betraying no confidences. Somebody in the village will tell you the story, more or less gleefully, more or less inaccurately, so you may as well get it right. The auditors found matter for amazement and concern in his books, which he had presumably expected a miracle to conceal. He had misappropriated clients' funds on a substantial scale. Nobody quite knows where the money went. It is locally supposed that he kept a girl in a maisonette in Milchester. This theory is not mentioned in the presence of his widow. I am telling you so that you will not be shocked when other people tell you, which, if you linger in these parts, they undoubtedly will. Anyway, he high-tailed it out of his office one jump ahead of the boys in blue, and went off for a sail in his little boat.'

'How miserable,' said Pippa.

'It was a terrible come-down, certainly. He had danced and pranced his way out of other jams, by dint of charm and so forth, and boasted about it afterwards, not so terribly attractive, not really quite sane. But this jam was too sticky. He could not dance out of trouble, so he sank. Some people might regard it as a cowardly way out. There are one or two retired admirals hereabouts who said he should have stayed and faced the music. I've always wondered what music they had in mind. The *Dead March*, perhaps. Personally, I'd rather be in prison than dead, but there's no accounting for tastes.'

The kettle boiled. Michael Craik made the coffee, as though he were host and Pippa the visitor. Drinking it, he looked at her with a kind of indifferent lechery.

When he left, he crossed the yard on to the lawn, and disappeared on foot through the garden. He made no sound. He went silently downhill towards the river. Pippa understood how he had got into the kitchen without her knowing it.

He had come into the kitchen at that hour hundreds of times. Probably he had started doing so when Judith Marriner was a young girl.

Everybody must have known about it in a place like this. Everybody knew everything in a place like this. No wonder Mrs Craik was a bit sour.

Nothing happened for an hour, absolutely nothing.

The telephone rang.

'It's late to be having gentleman callers,' said a sly, muffled voice. 'Yes, it's me again. Have you had word from your gracious hostess yet?'

'Mrs Marriner called.'

'From Italy?'

'Yes.'

'Modern science is wonderful. I hope she's having a lovely time.'

Pippa could think of no answer to this. She did not need one, because the caller rang off.

Pippa could make no sense of it all. She could see no reason for the call. The man must be near. He had seen Michael Craik — knew at least that he had come.

Another prowler, slinking through the paddocks, lurking in the stable or by the house, watching and listening. Why? What in God's name for?

The caller had confirmed that Judith Marriner was still away, that she was far away in Italy. He did achieve that.

Was that the idea, the single reason for the call?

Was he lurking and prowling and spying because Mrs Marriner was away? Why? Why? Why?

Pippa went to bed in the knowledge that, in the small hours, the dogs would bark like mad and she would hear a footstep on the gravel outside her window.

Was there anything she could do with this knowledge, any precaution she could take? The only thing she could think of was to sit up all night with lights blazing, to let the light stream out of the house from uncurtained windows. Well, she could do that. The Craiks over the valley would see the blaze of light, and think it odd, and tell a lot of people about it, and the prowler would see the light and keep his distance, and come back the next night, and nothing would be solved, only she would be short of sleep.

She would be short of sleep anyway. It was too much to expect sleep to come, when it was certain to be broken, when she was certain to be frightened.

She seemed to herself to have done nothing all day, but she found she was very tired.

She lay thinking not of Fenton Lowell, which was a relief, but of Jack Marriner going out alone in his dinghy, just ahead of the police — that was how it had sounded — unable to face the disgrace... Which would his wife have preferred? A husband alive but in prison? When she had just inherited this property, which must be one of the grandest hereabouts?

Judith Marriner had Mr Tomkins, who bored her, only because he was a gift. He was only a few months old. Who was he a gift from? The grateful neighbour who rode her horse, the childhood sweetheart from over the valley?

This was only a guess, but it was terribly likely.

All the girls were gooey about little Dan Mallett. Why was that?

Who was the oily, anonymous voice on the telephone?

Whose foot crunched the gravel in the middle of the night?

Pippa was in a little boat with Fenton Lowell, surrounded by seagulls. They were surprised by a storm of barking from the gulls.

Pippa woke painfully to the reality of barking; to the sound of footsteps on the gravel.

The prowler was not making much effort to be quiet. You could approach the house without sound — Michael Craik had done so. Why would anybody crunch about on the gravel, when there were grass and flagstones?

Pippa realized with a shock that this was a prowler who wanted to be heard. What on earth could be the point of that? To spoil her sleep, just for the sake of doing so?

Pippa tried to be angry in order not to be frightened, but it did not work very well.

The police, on the telephone in the morning, were profoundly unimpressed. They took Pippa's name and the names of the house and its owner; the officer who took the call probably added a note: 'Hysterical London female.'

The police pointed out that the driveway was a driveway, the gravel yard a place intended for the use of vehicles and pedestrians. It was for people's footsteps. Although it was private property, you could hardly say that anybody walking there was trespassing. There had been no damage? Nothing stolen? No litter left? No sign at all of any visitation? What exactly was it the caller was complaining of? A dog barking in the middle of the night? A dog in her own house, not the dog of a vexatious neighbour? Somebody had crunched the gravel? Was the gravel damaged? Did it even require raking?

What were the police supposed to do about it?

Pippa was made to feel a fool and a time-waster.

She went a different way with the dogs, in the early afternoon. She went across the road and down the hill towards the river. The squelching water-meadows were thronged with innumerable gulls, which seemed gradually to be moving westwards along the steel-grey line of the river, common gulls and black-headed gulls and the bigger, more aggressive herring gulls, none of them crying as they would have done over the sea or in a harbour, or in attendance on a moving ship, not using the wind as they would have done to fly with the extraordinary, effortless skill of their kind, but mooching about on the ground, and sometimes flying a little way, a great crowd brought together by chance, having no contact with one another, a huge number of isolated individuals like Londoners at lunchtime in the Strand, or commuters in Waterloo Station... Pippa was depressed to find herself being reminded of drab crowds of drab people, by these lovely and graceful birds.

She rejoined the road where it swung south to cross the river. There were half a dozen houses down here, and a warm-coloured mill by the bridge which had been turned into a fancy restaurant. A demure sign said that it was the Old Mill Restaurant. A yard paved with massive, uneven flagstones had dainty wrought-iron garden furniture and stone troughs in which, in the summer, there would be foaming aubretia. It was all in terribly good taste. Pippa's depression was increased, because it was the sort of place that made Fenton hoot with derision.

A side-road was signposted to 'Zelston Green only', and another sign said that there was no through road. Zelston Green must be, Pippa thought, about opposite Parsonage Farm, a mile or so away across the valley. If so, it was where the Craiks lived. Pippa told herself that she had no particular wish to inspect their house, and she was not sure what directed her up that side-road. It was a pretty little road. There was a fine view northwards over the valley, the ground rising above the water-meadows, plough and pasture and deep woods, and there also Parsonage Farm, distinctive with its fine outbuildings.

And here the road ended, simply died in a muddy puddle in the middle of a clump of little houses. Of these a couple were ancient cottages, four were newish, with car-ports and fancy iron lamps over the doors and satellite dishes in the gardens, and one, in a bigger garden, was a mock-Tudor horror of about 1930, a house which belonged on the Great West road on the way to a terrible factory.

A sign on the gate identified the Tudor house as Berryes, a name which seemed very odd to Pippa. This was the Craiks'. Yes, the strange little Dan Mallett had mentioned the name. Why was it the Craiks'? Why were such a couple in such a place — he one of the 'swift, indifferent men' who looked odd in anything except riding-boots, she a terrifying leather-hearted hunting virago from Leicestershire — what were they doing in a scrubby, suburban-looking little house in an acre of sour garden? She came from the Shires, so it was his. He had always been there, so it was his family's. It was his inheritance. This was Castle Craik.

No wonder he went to Parsonage Farm to ride Judith Marriner's horses.

Staring at the house, Pippa was suddenly aware that she was being stared at. She had thought the house lifeless, empty. It was not quite lifeless. There was somebody in an upstairs window, back from the window, fleetingly visible, alert, unfriendly.

Pippa felt acutely self-conscious, as though she had been caught at a keyhole. Then she thought: *they both bloody well came and spied on me, why shouldn't I have a look at them?* But when she turned from the gate and walked away down the road, she felt hostile, resentful eyes in the small of her back.

Berryes was a house with three or four bedrooms, no more. The downstairs rooms would be dark, with their low ceilings and phoney leaded windows. The doors and banisters would be gimcrack, lightweight, covered in nasty varnish; fitted cupboards would be made of plywood, and exposed beams stuck on. The only outbuilding was a garage with an asbestos roof. The garden was scrubby and sour, a rough lawn and overgrown shrubbery. Whoever lived in that house didn't care about it; their attention was elsewhere; they were either too busy to bother, or camping there in the expectation of better things.

It simply didn't go with the Craiks, with either of the Craiks.

Was it the best they could afford?

Did Michael Craik do anything? He looked and spoke as though he controlled broad acres, but he only had one broad acre, and he didn't trouble with that. He either spent a lot of money on whisky or else he had generous friends.

How did Mary Craik spend her days? Peeping out of upstairs windows? Or was that somebody else?

Pippa walked quickly and thankfully away from the place, from the ugly little huddle of houses. Even the dogs seemed cheered up; but that was because they knew they had turned homewards, towards their suppers.

There was no little man in baggy trousers, that evening, to look after the horses. Pippa assured herself that she was pleased. It was not a heavy task. Talisman the shaggy dun tried to bite her, and the full water-buckets were a fair weight.

Her chores completed, Pippa found herself wondering about Jack Marriner. Presumably they were right, the various things she had been hearing about him. Presumably Michael Craik was right. Was it a coward's way out? Was it better than disgrace, prison? Better for whom? Drowning was said to be a comfortable sort of death, but could it be? Going off the side of a boat deliberately? Not swimming, just letting go? Could one do that? Pippa thought instinct would have made one kick out, but perhaps the fear of disgrace was stronger than the instinct of self-preservation.

Was there any memory of him in the house, any sign of him, any souvenir? There was no drawing or framed photograph that could possibly be of him; there were no albums lying about; if he had won any medals or cups or certificates, they were not on display. Was he tall? Short? Dark? Fair? Bald? A gentleman? Always a crook or only that once? It was funny that a man should leave no imprint at all, even on his own environment, on the place where he lived. Of course, he had not lived here for long. And since he died in shame, in misery, his widow might have felt like erasing all trace of him, as Communist governments, once upon a time, rewrote history to expunge the memory of democratic heroes. Would Judith Marriner do that?

Could she? Could Pippa expunge the memory of Fenton Lowell?

At bedtime she wondered whether to sleep in a different room. She could go where there was no gravel outside the window. She decided there was no point in it. The dogs would wake her just the same. The unused bedrooms were chilly and gloomy. Judith Marriner's room was altogether too lush and scented, and Pippa had definitely not been expected to use it.

Pippa half wished, for once, that she had a sleeping pill.

81

The telephone had not rung. The dogs had not yet barked. It was quiet. It was too quiet.

Of course she lay awake. She lay in the darkness, trying not to listen but listening, waiting for the volley of barks from the kitchen, for the crunch of the footstep on the gravel.

Hour followed hour. The grandfather clock in the hall struck the hours and the quarters. She heard every one. She imagined she could hear the clock ticking through all the crawling hours of darkness.

She fell deeply asleep at last, and woke undisturbed in broad daylight.

Pippa felt a sense of anti-climax, which surprised her. She thought the dogs felt it too. Jacob went crossly all the way round the house, looking for the intruder who had not come.

Mary Craik's big shiny Volvo hummed up the drive in the late morning. It was hardly to be believed that this car belonged at the scrubby little house which Pippa had inspected. It was hardly to be believed that Mary Craik did either.

She glanced at the horses. She ignored the dogs. She would not come in. She wanted to know only if there had been a call, a message.

From whom? She would not say. Why a message for her here? She would not say.

It was something secret and guilty. It must be. Pippa did not want to be involved in other people's intrigues, and especially not in the intrigues of tough, bullying women she disliked.

Leaving, the Volvo nearly hit a bicyclist who was wobbling up the drive. Pippa gave a hiccup of dismay, because she thought the bicyclist was going to be hurt. It was Dan Mallett. Pippa reminded herself that she did not care a button about Dan Mallett, who was a notorious thief, and a great Don Juan among the local maidservants and shop girls, and impertinently thought he knew best about horses' diets…

And who did have, objectively speaking, the most remarkable blue eyes in the country, as well as a small, tough, rather elegant body discernible under those ridiculous clothes, and whose hands were narrow and oddly aristocratic, and who…

Anyway, he wobbled on up the drive unscathed. He climbed off his bicycle with a surge of treacly apologies for leaving Pippa to do the horses. He said he had been having trouble with his mother.

'A-ben fretful,' he said, 'come sprang o' th' year.'

'It isn't spring,' said Pippa.

'Next kin. If Janiveer be fine an' clear, we shall ha' winter half th' year.'

'Janiveer,' repeated Pippa stupidly, never having heard it before, rather liking the sound of it.

'A-ben talken wi' oldie worden,' said the ridiculous little man. He gave a sudden grin. It was broad, sweet, and unexpected. He was laughing at himself.

Pippa understood that among naive and inexperienced village girls, this little stoat could be a menace. But she was not going to be suckered, not again. She was once bitten; she was a burned child. She was in a position of responsibility. She was custodian of this property and of herself.

She said, 'I am perfectly capable of looking after the horses. Mrs Marriner is paying me to look after them.'

He grinned again. It was almost the same grin, but not quite. It was still tolerant mockery, but in a new direction. He was now not laughing at himself but at her.

His grin said that she was being pompous, priggish, toffee-nosed, hoity-toity.

Perhaps because she knew she was being these things, she became immediately and violently angry.

Pippa's anger and her pride ebbed with the daylight. The evening darkened the rooms of the house, rapidly and dolefully.

The dogs were restless.

'Hallo,' said a man's voice on the telephone at ten, a soft, cozening voice speaking as though with a mouthful of cotton wool.

'Yes?' said Pippa. 'Who is that? What do you want?'

He chuckled softly. The telephone clicked and buzzed. He had hung up.

Pippa knew that she, and the dogs, would once again hear the footsteps on the gravel in the small hours.

She was right.

Pippa heard something else, as well as footsteps, at a moment when the dogs had fallen silent. She heard a kind of laugh, a chuckle, a muffled snigger of derision. There was something triumphant about it, something boastful. It was the laugh of somebody congratulating himself, somebody who knew he was cleverer than anybody else. It was only a little snatch of sound, a fragile wisp, drowned immediately by the renewed uproar of all three dogs. It was impossible to identify with certainty. It was possible to interpret, perhaps — it was derision and a sense of superior cleverness, and there was a threat in it, and a note of idiocy.

Pippa thought it was the voice of the man on the telephone.

CHAPTER 6

The morning sun pretended that everything was all right. The dogs subscribed to this pretence. It was another March morning bizarrely dawning in January, full of the unseen presence of birds and buds and rising sap.

It was almost impossible to feel frightened on such a morning, to want to run away. But it could be done, and Pippa did it.

Dan Mallett had called her bluff. He left the horses to her, since she scorned his assistance. Perhaps he was simply busy somewhere else. Perhaps he was in prison again. Really this seemed the most likely. He did not look as if he was ever busy, or ever had been, or ever could be. But he made nothing of the weight of those big water-buckets.

One day he would be killed, wobbling about in the dark, without lights, on that ancient bicycle.

'You the young lady up Hodges'?' said the man in the garage. 'I should say Marriners', shouldn't I? Hodges' as was. Hodges' as wodges, hey, did you catch that as it flew by? I must tell Bert. Bert'll give birth to a set of spanners. Yes, we'll take the Visa. Anything else you require? We carries chockies, drinkies, fags, and a nice line of motoring accessories.'

He had stiff yellow hair and a dark pink face which looked as though stripped of one layer of skin. He wore big boots, but was otherwise thinly and poorly clad. Pippa thought he was not the owner of the garage, although he was pretending to be. 'Did you know Mrs Hodges?' asked Pippa.

She had not spoken to anybody since the previous evening. She wanted to reach out and touch anything human. She wanted her hand held, though not, perhaps, by the man in the garage.

'All me life,' he said, settling down for a nice long talk. 'I believe they come here jus' after the war. The rumble o' guns had ceased, the rattle of musketry. So all the bangs an' crashes come yere instead, along with their Royal Highnesses. I fell foul of them many a time, when I were a lad, for a nose drippin' in Sunday school, or one o' me socks down aroun' me ankle. Then along comes the Crown Princess, wi' no wish or intention to be cheeky.'

He was holding Pippa's credit card between thumb and finger, as though feeling the quality of the plastic.

'We all thought she'd marry that Craik, up Zelston. The Hodges thought so, an' the Crown Princess herself, she thought so, no desire to express meself impertinent. A match made in 'eaven, that seemed like, puttin' one thing alongside another.'

He paused. He stared into the distance. He was a man with nothing to do. The garage was on a quiet by-road. It was difficult to see how it survived. The man in charge was as bored and lonely as Pippa was. In features and in manner, and in style of talking, he bore some resemblance to the matting-haired woman in the newsagent's. It was likely enough that they were related. A remote place like this would be seething with kinships, acknowledged and unacknowledged.

'Mr Michael Craik, 'is trouble was 'e couldn't wait. When 'is dad died, there wasn't nobody to pay the bills. Shame, really. So it was go out an' seek a job o' work, or marry a lady wi' a sackful of brass. The latter of which 'e done, gainful employment, you understand, not bein' 'is cup o' tea.

Whereupon, the Crown Princess bein' throwed consequent into a dreadful takin', she up and married Mr Jack Marriner.'

'On the rebound,' suggested Pippa. She did not really despise herself for having this conversation, though her Pytchley aunt would have despised her for it.

'An' they all bin regrettin' it all round ever since, some more than others.'

'It often happens.'

'Leaving loose ends an' undiminished 'opes. You bin nurse-maidin' some o' them 'opes, retained in expectations o' golden futures. Exhaustin', I should 'azard a guess, lookin' after all them 'orses.'

'Dan Mallett does most of the work,' said Pippa, sure that the garage man would know him.

'If Dan Mallett ben liften a finger in honest toil,' said the garage man, 'then 'e 'as ulterior motives, bein', on the authority o' Police Constable James Gundry, upholder o' law an' order in this parish, the world's biggest villain unhung.'

Pippa nodded. She recovered her credit card at last. She said goodbye to her new friend and headed back to Parsonage Farm.

The horses and dogs were explained. It was explained why Michael Craik had married Mary, though not why Mary married Michael. Perhaps she had fallen in love with him. He jumped off his horse, after a hard day with hounds, and seduced her, whereupon she fell in love with him, and became putty in his hands.

Things did not happen like that.

With dismay, Pippa saw that things had happened exactly like that to herself. Fenton Lowell jumped off his chair after a hard day in the office, and seduced Pippa, with great ease and speed, whereupon etcetera. And she would have married him and gone to New York as readily as, presumably, Mary Craik had come to the nasty little house across the valley.

She wondered if men in garages discussed her affairs as freely as they discussed the Craiks and the Marriners.

Pippa fed herself, unhealthily, on bits and pieces. She walked the dogs and dealt with the horses, since Dan Mallett was continuing to call her bluff. She wondered how to get through another evening.

In the event, it was not without episode. Mary Craik was hit with the poker, then smothered with a cushion, while sitting by the telephone in the small sitting-room.

Pippa got the dogs out of the room. She shut the door on the corpse. She went to the other telephone in the hall by the front door. She opened the floodgates to people, noise, lights, confusion, suspicion, disbelief, men who needed shaves and deodorants, men who needed lessons in manners. The rest of the night was a vision of hell.

'We prefers a mornin' murder,' said one fat policeman. 'More considerate all round.'

A lot of things were immediately obvious, to Pippa and to the police.

Whoever tied Jacob up knew exactly what he was doing. He knew the house and the dogs. He knew that Jacob was the watchdog, that only Jacob of the three would stop him getting quietly into the house. He knew Jacob well enough to catch him and tie him up. He must have gagged or muzzled the little dog in some way. Probably he took him right away from the house and brought him back in time for the murder, in time to get Pippa away down the drive.

The telephone.

The telephone was as much the murder weapon as the poker and the cushion.

It seemed certain the murderer had made the call, or caused it to be made, in order to get Mary Craik to the killing ground, to the chair placed as though deliberately for this special purpose. The murderer knew all about that.

How did the murderer make that telephone call just then? Where from?

The murderer needed knowledge of the house and garden, the back door, the drive, the gate. He needed knowledge of Jacob, yes, and of the position of the telephone. That narrowed the field, no doubt about that, narrowed it to about six thousand people.

Everybody for miles around knew Jacob. The Hodges had had him as a young puppy. Now he was an old dog. He had been making a pest of himself in that neighbourhood for ten years or more.

The telephone in the small sitting-room had been in exactly the same place, on that desk, by that chair, since 1946, when Colonel Hodges had the extension put in. The Hodges were both intensely active in local affairs. That room was a study, a kind of office. Meetings and interviews of various sorts were held in it almost daily for something like forty years.

Motive? Nobody knew about any motive, not straight away.

The police took over the annexe as an Incident Room, assuming permission from Mrs Marriner which they were not at once able to secure. This arrangement gave them power, light, a separate telephone, all separately metered.

Jacob was incensed by all the activity, at policemen and pathologists and photographers, at vehicles and voices and the ringing of the telephone. He was still snapping at blue ankles at five in the morning.

In and out of the edge of Pippa's awareness, at various times during the interminable small hours, flickered Michael Craik, looking stunned, looking smaller than before, looking older.

One other face from the outside world came and went unobtrusively. It was Dan Mallett. He was 'helping the police with their inquiries'. This might mean what it usually meant, or what it literally meant.

Pippa was too sleepy to think, but one thing loomed up like a mountain through mists of sleep: it was obvious that Dan Mallett was the murderer.

He knew the place intimately well. He had known it all his life. He wasn't allowed inside the house, but that didn't mean that he hadn't been inside the house, that he wasn't inside it five times a week. He knew the dogs. Jacob knew him. Jacob seemed even to love and trust him. He could catch Jacob and tie him up. He was always prowling about, by day and by night, openly and secretly. No doubt he had an alibi for the night of the murder, and no doubt it was false.

All the girls were gooey about him. One of the girls would give him an alibi.

His motive was pretty obvious, too. Mary Craik knew he was a thief. She had said so. She had caught him at something. She was going to give him away. She was going to send him back to prison. He already had a record as long as his arm, short stretches for minor offences. Judith Marriner had said that. Probably this was something more serious. They'd send him up for a long time. Mary Craik would have been the chief prosecution witness. So he killed her before she laid the information, if that was what she was going to do.

If this was obvious to Pippa, it was presumably obvious to the police. In case it wasn't, did Pippa's civic duty oblige her to point it out to them? She thought not.

Was it Dan Mallett's footsteps she had heard on the gravel? His derisive snigger in the small hours?

There were other big questions unanswered.

Who had Mary Craik been expecting to see? She had been waiting for a message. She had evidently had a message: *Meet me at Parsonage Farm.* Meet who? Did he come? Did he kill her, rather than Dan Mallett? Why did he?

Pippa was questioned a second time and a third during the dragging purgatory of the following day. She was taken again and again through Mary's arrival, her excitement, the words which conveyed that she was expecting to meet somebody, to meet a man, to meet someone whom she could not meet in her own house. Pippa told again and again the story of Jacob's single bark, the telephone, the wire on Jacob's collar, the time the wire took to unravel.

Pippa did not know what time Jacob had disappeared, what time Mary Craik had arrived, how soon after that they had heard the barking of the dog, how long she had been out of the house. Compelled to guess, she guessed repeatedly, contradicting herself, becoming confused, made to feel unreasonably guilty.

She was taken again and again through the circumstances of her arrival at Parsonage Farm. She met Mrs Marriner for the very first time, as a complete stranger, at a function in London given by a person unknown to her, and within a week she was in sole possession of this large house and in sole charge of its valuable livestock? Miss Lees was advised to do better than that. The deceased, her husband, and Mrs Marriner were all quite often in London. Miss Lees would make things much easier for everybody, herself included, if she explained her connection with these people.

She denied any connection. She denied having heard of any of them ten days before. The police looked at her with cold, incredulous eyes.

There was no confirmation of her story about Jacob. There was no witness of her even having left the house, except Mrs Craik. There was no possibility of proving that she had gone to the bottom of the drive. She found and showed them the wire. She thought it proved something. They stared at it and at her. It was just a bit of twisted wire.

The telephone and fax were much in use. By evening, the police knew all about Pippa.

She had lost her job and she was homeless. Presumably she was desperate. The world was full of homeless unemployed people, and they were all naturally desperate.

She had been having a relationship (that was their word) with a tall, well-built man with fair hair, a healthy, powerful, well-dressed man some years older than herself, who struck their informants — a neighbour's daily cleaner, for example — as a very superior gentleman, quite the sort to be living in the country and riding horses.

What would her feelings be about this person's wife?

A policeman who knew about horses looked after the horses. Somebody took the dogs out on leads. Pippa was allowed to feed the dogs and herself, but she was not left alone.

She could not take seriously the idea that she was a suspect.

Footsteps on the gravel in the small hours of the morning? Mysterious telephone calls from an anonymous man with an ingratiating voice? Who says so?

The man she had been having a 'relationship' with was an American now returned to New York. Very convenient. Anyway, who said she could only have one relationship? The American was a married man who had gone back to his wife and children? Evidently she did not draw the line at having affairs with married men.

Mr Craik denied a relationship with Pippa. He would, wouldn't he? For his own sake as well as hers. It would all come out in the end.

'There may be mitigating circumstances,' said a Detective Chief Superintendent, 'but we shall only know about them if you tell us.'

Of course they were doing their best to get hold of Judith Marriner. They asked everybody who her friends might be in Italy, where she might have gone; they had the Italian police looking, with a description and a sheaf of photographs. But travel in Europe had become relaxed, informal. Nobody asked for a passport. You might tell where people had gone by their use of credit cards or Eurocheques, but unless they responded to a public appeal, you might never find where they were. It was obviously possible that Mrs Marriner had had a romantic assignation in Italy, in which case she might be discreet or even furtive; she might have dropped off the face of the known world into some inaccessible Umbrian farmhouse. Given all the circumstances, it was even probable that she had done so. She would not be seeing notices posted in municipal buildings.

All incoming calls would meanwhile be monitored. Pippa hoped they included a call from the man with the sinister voice. She hoped somebody would come to believe there was such a man.

She hoped that somebody, in the middle of the night, would hear a footstep on the gravel.

The police had not been interested when she first reported footsteps, because they thought it was unimportant. They were still not interested because they thought she had made it up.

Reporters became a pest of a kind which Pippa had hardly before imagined. She knew the press sometimes camped on your doorstep, if you were a girl who was said to be having an affair with a prince or a pop singer, but she had never imagined herself on the receiving end of the searchlight. There was one detestable fat man who wore his hat and smoked a small cigar in the drawing-room. Unfortunately, the police liked them. They kept giving statements and having press conferences, and they all wanted to be photographed. Only the Chief Superintendent was interviewed on television. Pippa had the impression that there was a good deal of resentment about this. She herself was photographed many times, but she was forbidden to say anything to the press.

Pippa overheard the journalists talking. They were sure Michael Craik had murdered his wife, but the law forbade them to say so. Mary had come to Parsonage Farm to meet a man. She would not, could not, perhaps dared not, meet him at home. She was excited. Michael found out about it. He killed her in a fit of jealous rage. As a scenario this was a bit ordinary but perfectly convincing.

Some of the reporters thought Michael and Pippa were accomplices, since they had been having an affair in London. They all hoped this was the case because it made such a beautiful story.

But nobody was yet arrested — not Michael, not Pippa, not Dan Mallett.

Forty-eight hours after the murder, and life remained a surrealistic nightmare.

Ordinary life was turned completely upside-down, but, most extraordinary of all, some strands of life continued as though nothing had happened. The birds and animals continued. In the stable, when Pippa went to tuck them up for the night, Cavendish and Dorothy greeted her with tolerant apathy, and Talisman made insincere efforts to bite her, exactly as always. Jacob came out with her as though bent on biting somebody, followed by Mr Tomkins falling over his feet and, reluctantly, by lazy old Bunbury. The bantams were all in bed, invisible in the hayloft; they chuckled in sleepy reproach when the light woke them up. In the aviary, the canaries and quails were fast asleep, unaware that a few yards away bloody murder was crying from the ground.

Nobody stopped Pippa. It seemed to be recognized that life had to go on — the life of the birds and animals, if not that of humans. But she had a notion that she was watched out of the house and would be watched back into it.

As once before, there was a light in the tack-room. It was no longer surprising or alarming or annoying. The police left lights blazing all over the place. It was probably wise, deterring snoopers and pilferers and ghoulish souvenir-hunters. The door of the tack-room was ajar. That was all right too — nobody would steal a saddle with half the county constabulary sitting outside the door.

A voice came from the tack-room. It was a man's voice, a pleasant, light voice which Pippa thought was familiar although she could not immediately place it. She was sure it was not a policeman's voice, nor a journalist's, thought she did not know why she was sure. It was a gentle voice, educated but with a pleasant touch of local burr.

The voice said, 'All his life he's been looking across the valley at this life, this house, this set-up.'

Pippa stood still, listening. She did not think she was eavesdropping, really. The sleepy movements of the horses, the shifting of their feet in the straw and on the cobbles drowned any small sounds she might have been making.

A woman's voice replied, a young woman's voice with a cool, expensive accent. She said, 'From what they all say in the village, he could have had it all.'

'Yes, but the timing was wrong. When his father died, he was skint. He didn't know where the next bottle of whisky was coming from. Judith didn't have any money of her own then, not till the old folk died. The poor fellow couldn't wait. Regular supplies had to be maintained. The hand on the tap ever turning, the pen flying over the cheque-book. The long-term future had to be sacrificed to the immediate necessity. He ate, in a manner of speaking, his seed-potatoes.'

'So now he'll get all this? Judith and the stables and the lot?'

'The prospect must have flickered through his mind, don't you think?'

'On the other hand,' said the woman, 'he has an alibi for the whole of the evening. He was in the pub. He was in the Chestnut Horse in the village.'

'There is a big objection to the theory that Michael Craik did it,' said the man. 'But his alibi's not it. That's only a minor objection. For one thing, the alibi might be phoney. You can't believe what people in pubs say, not the blokes in the Chestnut Horse. They wouldn't really have noticed whether he was there all the time or not. A man goes out for a slash, he could be gone half a minute or half an hour, they wouldn't remember. That's one possibility. The other is that he had a mate, and the mate actually did the bits with the poker and the cushion. Michael was an accessory before, during and after, but at the crucial moment he was actually in the Chestnut Horse. That's a serious possibility. It's how the bluebottles' minds are working.'

'How do you know?'

'I am an expert in the workings of the minds of the constabulary. They're often right but they're sometimes wrong, and this time they're wrong.'

'Go on.'

'My theory about which,' said the unseen man, 'would provoke incredulity, not to say derision.'

'Tell me, I won't mock.'

'Yes, you will. You think you won't, but you will. My solution to this mystery is simply too brilliant and amazing. The world is not ready for it. Groundwork needs to be carried out. Someone may even have to go abroad.'

'To find Judith Marriner?'

'No. She'll appear in due course, of her own accord. Somebody may have to go and find my murderer.'

'You are talking the most frightful rubbish. I must go. Thank you for the saddle. I'll bring it back next week, without fail.'

'Okay, love, no hurry. Nobody's riding these animals until they're shod.'

There were some farewells, affectionate but not passionate. There was nothing very private to hear, nothing embarrassing. Pippa had the strange impression that these two had once been lovers but were now friends; she did not know how she reached this peculiar conclusion.

A girl came out of the tack-room and out of the stables and away into the night. She did not notice Pippa, who was half hidden by Cavendish and in half-darkness. She was an extremely pretty girl a year or two older than Pippa, not unlike Pippa in appearance. Her hair was shorter than Pippa's and fairer, so fair it was almost white, her face perhaps broader, more childlike. She was wearing corduroys and a Husky, and carrying an old but expensive hunting saddle.

She was borrowing one of Judith Marriner's valuable saddles. Why was she? How dared she? Who had the bloody impertinence to lend such a thing to her? Who was the man in the tack-room, with what he said was an incredible theory about the murder, but one which would turn out to be true, with a gentle and educated voice with a slight and pleasing West Country burr? Who could he be?

Pippa stood still and quiet for a moment, looking over the withers of the tall horse, Cavendish, waiting for the intruder to come out.

Out of the tack-room came the man she least expected to see, a man who could not have been speaking with the voice Pippa heard. It was a trick of the light. The evidence of her senses was not to be believed.

Dan Mallett came out of the tack-room, turned off the light, locked the door, put the key away in its hiding place, and followed the fair girl away into the darkness.

CHAPTER 7

Pippa's first idea was to unlock the tack-room and find out who had really been talking to the girl. The poor man had somehow allowed himself to be locked in there by Dan Mallett. This idea went almost as soon as it came. Nobody was locked in the tack-room. Everybody who had been in the place had come out of it. The fact had to be faced, stranger than all the other things she had faced. There was more to Dan Mallett than met the eye. There was altogether too much.

He had a theory about the murder which nobody would believe. Would he be likely to have a good theory? How was he to be judged, as a framer of theories about murders? As anything? What was he? Who was he? How did anybody come by two such different personalities? Did he have others? How many? What was, or had been, between him and the fair girl? Who and what was she? Why, as to that, should Pippa give a damn?

There was one thing that could be said about Dan Mallett, one thing in his favour — there had been one thing that could have been said about him. His voice could not possibly be — could not possibly have been — the creepy voice on the telephone. That voice was odd and unpleasant, but it was educated. It was not the voice of a half-literate peasant.

This was no longer true. The one thing in Dan Mallett's favour was not in his favour any longer. There was nothing in his favour.

He lent other people's expensive saddles to fair-haired tarts who came slinking deceitfully into the stable in the middle of the night.

He wouldn't have the gall to do that, perhaps, if he had murdered Mary Craik. But he might do it because he'd murdered Mary Craik, bluffing, showing the confidence of the innocent.

Was that the theory that nobody would believe, that he himself had done it? Would anybody talk like that? Why would he have to go abroad to find himself, when he was here on the spot already...?

The police were slow to turn their attention to the burglar alarm, but when at last they examined it, they did so thoroughly.

'When and why,' they said to Pippa, 'did you disable the alarm?'

'I don't know how it works,' said Pippa. 'I don't know where the switches are, or anything about it. Mrs Marriner never mentioned it.'

They looked at her sadly, and telephoned. Presently a young man in pink trousers appeared in a pink van on the side of which was lettered 'Harlequin Home Security'. Yes, his company had installed the alarm eighteen months before and had twice serviced it since. It was, or had been, in perfect working order. It had now been not merely switched off but sabotaged. It could be repaired, but the cost would be substantial. The company would submit an estimate. No doubt Mrs Marriner would contact them on her return.

The sabotage was not the crude hacking of cables from outside, but delicate destruction inside. The fault had not been easy to find and would not be easy to fix.

Whoever had done the damage knew the house and the installation.

The alarm had last been serviced the previous June. The damage could therefore have been done at any time in those seven months. People with the necessary entree and the necessary knowledge of the house could include electrician, plumber, decorator, rat catcher, daily cleaner, carpet-layer and a dozen other servants and tradesmen, together with an unknown number of visitors, friends, house-guests or intruders. The plan could have been a robbery in July, the culprit a window cleaner in the pay of a Milchester crook, the burglary aborted for any of a thousand reasons; it could all be completely unconnected with the murder.

But it was difficult to think so.

The thing was so obvious that it hung in the air like a lamp between Pippa and the policemen. The alarm had been sabotaged for the same reason Jacob had been neutralized and probably by the same person.

Probably Dan Mallett knew all about that alarm; as he certainly knew all about Jacob.

If he did the murder, nobody would ever know exactly why.

He did not look strong enough to hit anybody on the head and then asphyxiate them. But Pippa had seen him carry two big, brim-full stable buckets without any apparent distress, without a break in his ridiculous treacly voice. He was strong all right, even if he did look like an archaic waif in clothes too big for him.

After the pink van disappeared down the drive, Dan Mallett wobbled up it.

The police never seemed to notice that he rode his bicycle without lights. They did not much notice him at all. He came and went as if he were invisible.

Pippa saw the light from the stables. He was getting the feeds ready. Then he would bring the horses in. Pippa was no nearer understanding why he did it.

Pippa had been mildly curious about this local leprechaun. Since hearing him the previous evening, talking to that needlessly pretty fair girl, she had become obsessed by curiosity.

How could there be two such different people inside that one small person? How could a man speak with two such voices? Why did he? Did he kiss the fair girl? What were they to one another? What had they been? Did he murder Mary Craik? Where did he live? How? With whom?

Every evening he wobbled away into the darkness, into some unknown land from which he seduced all the girls for miles around, and stole everything not nailed down.

Snipe-like and uncertain as was his course on his bicycle, Pippa could not follow him on foot. She could not follow him in her car.

She suddenly realized what she could do. The thought made her give a sudden snort of slightly hysterical laughter, which caused a massive uniformed constable to stare at her with pitying disapproval.

Pippa shocked and astonished herself by sticking out her tongue at the policeman.

She slipped out of the house, into the gathering darkness of the yard. She was unnoticed, unchallenged. She found Dan Mallett's ancient bicycle leaning where he had left it behind the corner of the stable. She saw that he had no pump. She would have been astonished if he had had anything as fancy as lights or bell or pump. She doubted if he had any brakes.

The tyres of the bicycle were pneumatic and they had air in them. They had normal valves, the one on the back wheel even protected by its little screw cap.

Pippa got a nail from the tool shed. With the point of the nail, she pressed down the little spike in the middle of each valve so that all the air in both tyres came hissing miserably out. The noise sounded loud enough to be heard in London, but perhaps not in the stable over the noise of all three horses chomping their oats and nuts.

Even Dan Mallett would not ride a bicycle with both tyres completely flat.

Pippa waited for him to finish with the horses. She kept an eye on the golden windows of the stable, which she could do without being obvious about it.

While she waited, she thought about what she had heard.

The manner of Dan Mallett's conversation had so astonished her that she had not considered the matter of it. She pondered it now.

Michael Craik, all his life, had stared across the valley from his family's nasty little house at this nice big one; from an acre of scrub at a big, beautiful garden and ample paddocks, and horses in the stable, and the life of a country gentleman. He was a kind of gentleman himself, by education and accent, so he knew what he was looking at.

He wanted it.

He yearned and slavered and slobbered for it. He could have had it. He must have been tortured by that thought. He could have had Judith Duxbury, the dainty little heiress, and all that she inherited, the wealth and the way of life, the beasts and birds and antique furniture and cellar of wine.

But he had to have the bills paid, not tomorrow but today. So he married the woman with the big nose and thin lips, the yapping voice and the barking laugh, and she paid for the whisky and the central heating.

And Michael Craik knew the dogs. No doubt he had given Mr Tomkins to Judith. He knew Jacob. He could catch and quieten the old thing, if anybody could.

He knew where the instant coffee was. Obviously he knew all about the burglar alarm. He could have put that out of action the evening that he came, when Pippa was in the stable, or before she arrived on that first morning, or at any of a thousand moments over the previous months.

He lured his wife to this house, to the Marriners', with the promise that she would meet somebody. A lover. That was how Mary Craik had behaved — a bit drunk and excited and feeling sexy. It was somebody she could not meet at home. She said that. She could only come to Parsonage Farm if Judith Marriner was away. Michael Craik had said that.

Who could Mary Craik's lover be? What kind of man would want her? How was it possible?

Had Mary Craik bought a lover as well as a husband?

Pippa felt a bit ashamed of thinking in these intolerant terms of somebody recently and violently dead; but the fact did remain — it was extremely hard to imagine a man wanting a passionate involvement with Mary Craik.

Pippa tried to shut her mind to some of the farcical and obscene speculations which these thoughts summoned.

She tried to shut her mind to speculation about Dan Mallett and the very pretty fair girl who had taken away the saddle.

The unpleasant voice on the telephone was muffled, disguised. It was an educated voice.

It was Michael Craik's voice.

Michael Craik had an alibi for the whole of the evening of the murder. Did he, though?

Judith Marriner inherited, and then she was widowed. Michael Craik, still staring with passionate envy across the valley, saw Judith rich, Judith in possession of everything he wanted, Judith free and available. She really was available. She was caretaking all these things she did not want for herself, these dogs and horses and old armchairs; she was keeping them warm for him, for Michael Craik. She wanted him. The welcome mat was out for him. So why murder anybody? Why didn't Michael Craik slam the door behind him, go down the hill and across the river and up the other side, and simply move in with Judith? He didn't need Mary's money anymore, because he could have Judith's. Anyway, Judith had more. Mary could once upon a time have refused to give Michael a divorce, but nowadays he could get one anyway; and that was even supposing these people would be bothered with refinements like marriage and divorce.

Mary had some kind of hold over Michael, maybe over Judith. Michael could not have Judith, and all that was hers, until Mary was removed, blown away.

Yes. It was something like that.

It was certainly something exactly like that.

Everything Pippa had learned, that had got her to this point, was obviously known to the police; everything she had heard from the woman in the newsagent's and the man in the garage and Michael Craik himself, everything she had overheard from Dan Mallett, all of this was available stuff. So the police already knew, or were trying to find out, what power Mary Craik had had over her husband and his girlfriend.

How do you have power over people, in a situation like that? Was Michael Craik a drug addict, a pervert? Could Mary have shopped him for theft, rape, buggery? Could she have shopped

Judith Marriner for anything? Holding this over their heads to keep them in line?

All the police had to do was to find it. Pippa hoped they knew what they were supposed to be looking for. She was pleased with herself that she had worked it all out so tidily.

Michael Craik, intermittently visible, hanging about and answering questions, did not act like a man who had just done a murder. No, indeed. He was very carefully acting like a man who had not done a murder, who was shattered and appalled by the death of his wife.

Acting was the word. He would, wouldn't he?

Michael Craik and Dan Mallett had known one another all their lives. Dan Mallett had done odd jobs for Michael Craik's mother; Michael and Dan had both been coming to Parsonage Farm, off and on, for years. Michael Craik might have a genuine alibi for the night of the murder. All he needed was an old friend who was also a friend of the dog Jacob.

Pippa saw that it was more than ever vital that she knew where Dan Mallett went, when he wobbled away in the dark on his bicycle.

Only this evening he would be walking.

Pippa was watching from the window of the downstairs back passage, which gave on to the yard and the stables. She thought she saw Dan Mallett's shadow moving in the golden oblongs of the stable windows; but it might have been one of the horses moving, or a bantam sleepily going upstairs or downstairs. She could not see the bicycle in the darkness of the yard, but she knew where it was.

She had a coat ready to hand, and sheepskin mittens and a woolly hat. She thought that if she put them on she would look and feel absurd. She did not think a policeman would stop her dressing up and going out. She could say something about the horses. The police knew that Dan Mallett was looking after the horses, but they also knew that Pippa was being paid to do so, or said she was. She thought Dan Mallett would not immediately go rushing away down the drive, with or without his useless bicycle. He would prod the tyres and mutter to himself and scratch his head, and probably look for a bicycle pump in the shed. It would give Pippa time to get into her coat and out of the house.

Then it was simply a question of following where he led.

Supposing it was too far to walk? Then Dan Mallett would not try to walk it. Would he then hitch a lift with the police, or sleep in the stable, or what? If he did those things, nothing would be gained by the gambit of the bicycle tyres, but nothing would be lost.

A little bit was gained by letting the air out of those tyres. It was a tiny victory. It was the only thing approaching a victory Pippa had had since she came to this place; the only thing since Fenton Lowell went back to America; the only thing since before she ever met Fenton.

She hugged to herself her single achievement: letting the air out of the tyres of a small impoverished peasant.

The yellow oblongs disappeared from the wall of the stable. The light from the windows of the house was now more clearly visible, badging the flagstones of the yard, catching the chrome on the bumper of a police car. The light went out in the tack-room. A small figure in large clothes appeared in the door. There was a bit of fiddling with bolts and latches.

Dan Mallett pulled his ancient bicycle from the deep shadow where it spent the evening. He wheeled it a few feet away from the wall, to a place where he could conveniently mount. It was enough. He realized something was wrong. He crouched by the bicycle, prodding the tyres. He wheeled the bicycle to the door of the stable. The bicycle went uneasily over the flagstones, as though limping. He opened the door and turned on the light inside. He could now examine the flat tyres. He looked at them and at the valves. He squatted by the back wheel of the bicycle. He appeared to be pondering. Pippa had the impression that he was counting on his fingers, doing some primitive calculation.

He rose to his feet. He walked with a briskness Pippa had never seen him use, out of the yard and out of her sight. He was going to the door of the annexe, where the police had their temporary headquarters. He was going to report the outrage to the police. Or ask for the loan of a pump. Or cadge a lift.

He might still walk away down the drive. Pippa might follow. Nothing happened for dragging minutes, in the yard or in the house. The wounded bicycle stood in the dim light from the stable, like a victim in a Goya engraving of a casualty of war.

There was a buzz from the back door, by the kitchen — some piece of electric communication put in by the police to save themselves a few yards of walking. Pippa heard a murmuring voice, and another. Then there were footsteps on the flagstones, and a voice said, 'Miss Lees?'

'Here,' said Pippa. She knew what this was about. She was suddenly aghast at what she had done.

It was the Detective Sergeant, the one with the big white face like a Hereford bullock. Pippa knew it was a Hereford the Sergeant was like, because for a few years her father had tried to make money out of his paddocks by fattening bullocks for the market. Those bullocks were gentle and inquisitive. This Sergeant who resembled them was just as inquisitive but not so gentle.

'We has a nasty little specimen here, Miss Lees,' said the Sergeant, 'name o' Mallett, jus' made a ridiculous allegation.

The rules oblige me to go through the motions of treating it serious. All you require to do is issue a formal denial. Simply state in the presence of meself and the constable here, him actin' as witness, that you did not deliberately and wi' malice tamper wi' Dan Mallett's bike.'

Pippa opened her mouth to tell a lie and shut it again, not being a ready liar.

Behind and below the Sergeant — almost in his armpit, as it were — appeared a small wedge-shaped face, deeply tanned, with startling blue eyes. The face wore a look of gentle reproach. It was a ridiculous expression for that of all faces to wear.

'All 'at a-ben beggen,' said Dan Mallett, in a voice even more than usual like molasses, 'ben a liftie t'home wi' motor.'

'He thinks, or purports to think,' said the Sergeant, 'that as you disabled his bicycle, you ought to give him a ride.'

'Ben a tidy step, long o' Shank's pony,' said Dan Mallett.

'All right,' said Pippa. She made her voice reluctant, but she was delighted. She could find out about Dan Mallett without anybody realizing that that was what she was doing; she could also appease her conscience in the matter of the bicycle tyres without making any admissions.

'I don't mind giving him a lift,' she said, 'if you don't mind me going off in my car.'

'We trusts you t' come back, miss,' said the Sergeant, 'in the knowledge that the dogs depends on you for food, walks an' home comforts. 'Sides, you couldn't do a bunk, not in this weather, not with nowhere to bunk to.'

Pippa put on the coat and hat and gloves that she had ready for a different kind of expedition; she put on as much dignity as she could.

Dan Mallett bowed her through the door, as only he and Fenton Lowell had ever done.

Pippa had the idea that, as she went through the door, Dan Mallett and the Sergeant winked at one another behind her back. She could not be sure about this, since, if it occurred, it occurred out of her sight. But the impression was strong.

She was not manipulating anybody. After all the trouble she had taken, she was being manipulated. This notion made her very cross.

In this matter of the lift in her car, she was being subjected to moral blackmail by a notorious local villain, who was probably an accessory to murder.

Dan Mallett held the car door for her. He pretty nearly bowed.

She started the car as he climbed in. She switched on the lights and gave the engine a moment to warm up.

She said, 'Why did you think I let the air out of your tyres?'

He said, 'Why do you think that's what's wrong with my bike?'

'Because you said... The Sergeant said... Oh.'

'I didn't think the bluebottles had done it. I didn't think it was the reporters or the photographers. I was pretty sure it wasn't me. That only left you.'

Pippa put the car into reverse with a sickening crunch, owing to her embarrassment. She did not quite back into the police car which was parked in the yard. It was the kind of evening when she was liable to hit a gatepost.

Dan Mallett did not seem to expect her to say anything. This was lucky, as she could not think of anything to say.

They were halfway down the drive when she realized that it was not Dan Mallett who had been talking, who was sitting placidly beside her in the car. It was the well-spoken, educated stranger who was freakishly identical to Dan Mallett, the one who had lent the expensive saddle to the girl with straw-coloured hair.

'Who's that girl with fair hair?' said Pippa, words coming out of her mouth which she had not at all intended.

'Ah?' said Dan Mallett, as though uncertain which of many fair-haired girls Pippa meant.

'The one who took the saddle.'

'*That* one. Old and valued friend. Guaranteed to return borrowed merchandise in good order.'

'How many other voices have you got?'

'Not many. Variations on a theme. Go right along the road, towards the village, if you're really taking me home.'

'I seem to be.'

'What actually possessed you to fool about with my poor old machine?'

Well, what had? Now that she looked back on it soberly, Pippa baffled herself. She had been motivated by curiosity about Dan Mallett, so much she understood; but why had she been? Because she thought he was a murderer? Did she think so now?

Dan Mallett directed her, in his pleasant, educated voice, into and through the village of Medwell Fratrorum, past the church and a pub called the Chestnut Horse, across the river which she had crossed five miles upstream, and into a dark quiet wilderness of big trees fleetingly lit by the headlights, and tall unkempt hedgerows and drunken gates.

It seemed to Pippa that narrow golden eyes gleamed from the verge and from the lower branches of the trees, and that whispers followed them. She was being taken into a world she did not know. She felt like Mole in the Wild Wood.

They turned off the road onto a track, and crawled along the edge of a wood by Arthur Rackham. Pippa tried to steer between potholes. She drove in bottom gear, at a walking pace. Dan Mallett sat peacefully beside her, possibly humming almost inaudibly.

Suddenly there were undoubted eyes in the headlights, a pair of magical golden eyes, two pairs, three. There was a volley of barking.

'Greetings from the wolf-pack,' said Dan Mallett. 'Thank you very much for the lift.'

Pipa stopped the car. She could just see now, at the very edge of the glow of the headlights, a cottage which seemed to be stuck to the edge of the woods like a nesting-box in a garden, with no vertical, and the roof beetling down over the upstairs windows as though too big for the house.

In the cottage, Pippa knew, was a senile, pathetic, disgusting old woman, witless and dirty and dribbling, Dan Mallett's mother. Judith Marriner had sufficiently described her. Judith had not described the dogs, because she was not interested in dogs, even her own. Obviously these yapping dogs were mangy underfed mongrels, vicious and diseased. It was all an aspect of life in the English countryside which Pippa had never seen — something unknown in the tidy Oxfordshire village of her childhood — an ancient, uncouth, frightening world which should have been swept away centuries ago.

It fitted the Dan Mallett of the baggy trousers and the antique, treacly voice. It fitted his reputation and his prison record. But it was utterly incongruous with the voice she had just been hearing. What was he really? Who was he? He kissed her. It was a good, smacking, positive kiss, but gentle. His lips were dry and warm. 'A bids ye peaceable slumberen,' he said in his treacly voice. The next thing she knew, he was gone.

CHAPTER 8

Dan Mallett disappeared, presumably into the house, if you could call it a house. Pippa did not see him; she did not hear him, over the maniac barking of the dogs.

Pippa pictured the interior of the cottage, cramped and greasy, with scraps of mouldering carpet on a floor of ancient filth, windows never opened, their glass fly-blown and festooned with cobwebs, a few sticks of rickety furniture, unwashed tin plates and chipped enamel mugs, the air a fog from stolen coal in the grate and fried food and the steam of dirty clothes and dirty bodies, and in the midst of the squalor the obscene and pitiable ruin of the old woman…

The smell must be awful.

It was a bloody outrageous liberty, suddenly kissing her. They said in the village that no girl could resist him. He thought so. Enough silly little simpering shop girls had told him so. Nothing was more irritating, sick-making, contemptible than a man who thought he was irresistible.

How had such a funny little peasant come by that other way of talking?

Angry and puzzled and confused by the barking of the dogs, Pippa turned the car and bumped slowly back up the line to the road. She stopped at the corner, before pulling out into the road.

A voice came from behind her, from the darkness of the back seat.

The voice said, 'Don't turn right. Don't let's go home yet. We've got one or two things to talk about.'

It was the voice of the midnight telephone. It was a smooth, knowing, smarmy voice, educated but unpleasant, somehow muffled, as though the speaker had a handkerchief in his mouth.

Pippa screamed.

'Yes, if you like,' said the voice. 'I don't mind. I rather like the noise of a girl screaming. Nobody can hear you. There's half a mile of jungle between us and the Malletts' cottage, and the dogs are probably still barking. Can you feel this?'

His voice was suddenly close behind her, his mouth inches from the back of her neck.

She felt a prick, like the point of a pin, in the flesh of her neck just below and behind her left ear.

She screamed again, but it came out a higher and thinner scream, more of despair and fright than of surprise.

'It may feel like a needle, but it's a knife,' said the voice. 'It's actually just a kitchen knife, but it's awfully sharp. The blade's about eight inches long. I wonder what they'll think, when they find you without a head? Ever so astonished, they'll be. They'll think it's because you were nosing about in things that didn't concern you, and they'll be right. It's become a dangerous thing to do, what you've been doing, asking questions and talking too much.'

'Who are you?' said Pippa, in a voice that sounded to herself pathetically tiny and terrified.

'Don't be silly. We're old friends, you and I. Pen-pals, as it were, except we use the telephone. You hear my footsteps dancing on the gravel at midnight, at least I'm told you say you hear somebody's footsteps.'

Whose voice was it? Did she know the voice, from anywhere besides the telephone? Was it somebody she saw and spoke to by daylight? It was disguised by somebody who knew how to disguise his voice, who was brilliant at it, who already had more than one voice…

Could he have got out of the car and got in again?

Maybe yes, in the dark, with the noise the dogs were making, with the engine grinding in reverse, with her own confusion and distraction after that damned kiss…

Was that why he did it? He kissed her in order to distract her, so that he could climb into the back of her car?

'As soon as I knew you were using the car this evening, I hopped aboard like a rabbit,' said the nasty voice behind her. 'I didn't have to wait long. I thought it was a good way to be sure of talking to you alone.'

Pippa thought that, if she suddenly turned her head, she might see the face which was so close behind her. She was frightened. The point of the knife was very sharp. She did not try to visualize the knife, but she easily visualized it without trying to. Tentatively, she twitched her head a little round to the left. It was a movement which could be part of turning into the road.

Instantly she felt an urgent, a more violent pin-prick.

'Eyes front,' said the hated voice, 'or you'll have us in the ditch.'

'Where shall I go?' said Pippa, with extreme difficulty.

'Quietly along this road until I tell you to stop. Don't stop until I tell you. Don't even think of stopping if you see somebody on foot, or another car, or anything you think I might not like. That's fine. Twenty-five miles an hour is just fine. I want you to understand that I know everything about you, and I know everything you do, and who you talk to, and what you say. I want you to remember that I have this knife. Remember what the point feels like. Keep remembering that, and remember not to do anything that I might not like. I think you know what I mean. Just remember the knife, and don't do anything you think I might not like. You probably think I'm trying to scare you. You're right. And I think I'm succeeding. Stop now. Thank you for the lift. Drive on immediately you hear my door shut. Don't try to look back, and don't turn round until you get to the next crossroads. Do exactly what I tell you, now and henceforth, or I shall cut your head off with this knife.'

The car had stopped. The back door opened and closed.

Pippa tried and failed to see anything in the rear mirror over the windscreen. She could see nothing in the dark in the wing-mirror. She did not dare turn round to look; if the owner of the voice were watching, he would see her movement, perhaps, in the glow of the instruments in the dashboard.

Over the mutter of the engine, she did not hear his footsteps on the road or the grass of the verge. She did not know if he was a big man or a little one, or what he usually sounded like.

She did not know if she should report the business to the police. They would think she should. It was easy for them to think that. The owner of the voice would know that she had reported it, and he would cut her head off.

She drove back to Parsonage Farm feeling very cold and small and scared.

Poking and prying? Asking questions? Sticking her nose into other people's business? Had she been doing these things?

Maybe a bit. This place was mysterious even before the murder. It was reasonable to be curious. She didn't have to ask many questions. People told her things. The woman in the newsagent's, the man in the garage, Michael Craik, Mary Craik herself. Only Judith Marriner had told her absolutely nothing.

Dan Mallett had told her practically nothing, but she had overheard him talking to the fair girl.

Somebody who was looking and listening might get the impression she was prying. Apparently that was what had happened. The man had got that impression — the man on the telephone, the man with the knife. He had been on the spot, watching the house, watching her. He thought she was snooping. He warned her to stop. He threatened to cut her head off. He sounded as though he meant it. Why? He had a large and dangerous secret.

Obviously he had murdered Mary Craik.

'There you are, miss,' said the Sergeant with the face like a Hereford bullock. 'Took you a time taking that Mallett home.'

'Yes,' said Pippa.

There was a meaty Woman Police Constable standing in the doorway behind the Sergeant. She looked at Pippa. It was a pretty keen darting sort of look, appraising Pippa, wondering what she'd been up to, wondering if she was any good at it.

The Sergeant glanced back over his shoulder at the WPC. He seemed to wink. It was his evening for seeming to wink.

For a moment, Pippa was angry enough to forget to be frightened.

Mr Tomkins, the King Charles spaniel, told Pippa that the man did not mean it about cutting off her head with his knife. Jacob, the dachshund, snapped that, on the contrary, he did mean it. Old Bunbury could not have cared less.

The horses were apathetic. They had wisps of hay in their forelocks. Talisman, the dun, had somehow got his stable-rug askew. Pippa loosened the surcingle in order to straighten the rug over his quarters; he made his usual insincere attempt to bite her.

All this was blessedly normal. It should have been more comforting than it was. Talisman's old yellow teeth did not dislodge the memory of the needle-sharp knife-point.

It was the world's easiest house to prowl round, to spy on and eavesdrop and snoop. Trees grew near it, shrubs right up to it. There were all those rambling outbuildings. There were many large ground-floor windows. There was a five-room annexe. There were outside lights, but only two, and most of the exterior of the house was in total darkness, however many lights were blazing indoors.

But it was complicated. The immediate surroundings of the house were full of traps in the dark.

And there was Jacob.

It came to this. It was an easy house to spy on for anybody who knew it really well, and whom Jacob knew really well.

He could have got the sharp kitchen knife from anybody's kitchen, or from a shop.

Hours later. The house was silent. The dogs were asleep, Jacob twitching and Bunbury gently snoring. The policemen camped in the annexe were eating or sleeping or studying. The horses and bantams were quiet, and the canaries had their heads under their wings.

Pippa felt herself alone in the world, the single survivor of disaster, of a visitation which had killed or stunned all other living creatures.

She found a packet of runner beans in the freezer, to go with the fillet of haddock she found there. She read the directions. (In the life she had had before this life, she had been taught to eat only fresh vegetables, at whatever cost.)

You cooked the things from frozen, but you took them out of the packet first. The packet was made of tough plastic.

Obviously one wanted scissors. There were kitchen scissors, oddly shaped, asymmetrical, with jaunty orange handles. They usually hung on a pegboard beside the stove, with such other utensils as had holes in their handles. The scissors were not needed for every meal, but they were needed whenever a plastic envelope had to be slit open.

The scissors were not on their peg.

Pippa might have taken them out of the kitchen. She might have wanted them to cut the binder-twine round a new bale of hay. But there was a knife in the tack-room specially for cutting the string on haybales. Pippa was sure she had not taken the scissors out to the stables. She had not taken them into the small sitting-room, or the large one, or upstairs. She had not opened a packet of anything in any other place than this.

Somehow, the scissors had got into a drawer. This was practically impossible, but it was what must have happened.

Pippa began to go through the drawers in the various cabinets in the old kitchen.

There were scores of knives, and openers and corkscrews and small steel tools and implements of unguessable function, and skewers and candle-holders and napkin rings, and spatulas and wooden spoons and ladles and cotton reels and balls of string, and small batteries for flashlights or calculators, and useless flashlights and two useless calculators, and matches and candles and tape measures and nails, packets of thirteen-amp fuses, short lengths of electric flex, ancient crumbs, the lids of jam jars...

And a packet of photographs, two dozen colour prints and strips of 35 millimetre negative. Looking at somebody's photographs was not like looking at somebody's letters. Photographs were meant to be looked at. It was what they were for.

Pippa put the packet on the kitchen table. Finding it was the only good thing that had happened to her since the middle of the afternoon.

Then the next good thing happened, which was that she found the scissors. They were under the photographs.

It was not somewhere that the scissors could possibly be, but it was where they were.

Pippa had an aunt called Rosemary Gordon. Aunt Rosemary formulated Gordon's Law, which was roughly that the thing you wanted was always at the back of a drawer, and it was always the wrong drawer. She had been talking about her reading-glasses, but it applied to kitchen scissors. Unseen forces, tiny but malignant, hid them under packets of photographs in kitchen drawers, the wrong kitchen drawers. Bully for Aunt Rosemary.

It was the sort of thing there was no explanation for. It was no good looking for one. The strange location of the scissors was not strange, but normal. Aunt Rosemary said so.

Pippa put the haddock on a dish in the oven. She put some water in a saucepan for the beans. She sat down to look at the photographs, remembering with mild astonishment that these were the first photographs she had seen in this house that were less than fifty years old. She would have expected pictures of children in many households, or of dogs or horses. Here she thought she expected holiday snaps.

They were holiday snaps.

But they were the wrong holiday snaps. They were not only in the wrong place, they were pictures of the wrong people. They were middle-aged people in silly shirts. They were having drinks outside cafes in the sun, they were having picnics, they were standing by cars. They wore sunglasses and their skins were mauve from the sun. There was a fattish man with a ginger moustache, who always waved his cigarette at the camera. The setting was France, but it was not the Riviera. There were Dubonnet posters, but no pine trees. In the distance of some seaside photographs there were clutches of neat white houses with black slate roofs. The trees were broad-leaved and the grass was green. Pippa thought the people were in Brittany. This was confirmed by a couple of tall lace caps in a picturesque market.

There were four people in the photographs — another man, thinner and dark, and not working so hard at having a happy time; a beefy woman with a narrow mouth; a small, faded blonde. It was not obvious which person went with which. Evidently they had taken turns with the camera. A few photographs showed all four; they did as people often do, and got a waiter to take a photograph.

And then, towards the bottom of the pile, another character joined the cast: a tough, fox-hunting-looking woman in her forties, with big features and scarlet lips and a tight black perm. She looked awful, in flimsy holiday clothes. This character's presence explained why the photographs were in this part of England, though not in this house. It was Mary Craik.

Pippa riffled quickly through the dozen remaining colour prints, expecting to come on the coarse, handsome face of Michael Craik, and his powerful physique displayed in shorts or swimsuit. But he was not there. It was possible, of course, that he had been holding the camera whenever his wife was in the frame, but this seemed unlikely. He was keeping the home fires burning, or having another holiday somewhere else.

Was Mary alone with these two other couples? A single room in those little seaside hotels, among the rocks and grassy knolls and French families?

There were one or two other faces which made fleeting appearances in the photographs — faces which belonged in the pictures, so to speak, as opposed to waiters or *petits bourgeois* on holiday — but they might have been chance-met English, or even not met at all, but included in the frame by physical accident. The faces meant nothing to Pippa. There were none very handsome or very ugly, very young, old or odd. There was no face that explained why these pictures were in the house.

There was no reason to suppose that Pippa had discovered anything. Michael Craik must have known that his wife had been on holiday in France, in what must have been the last two or three years. Presumably he knew who her companions were. He must have seen these photographs, his wife's holiday snaps. Almost certainly it was he who had brought them here, which must have been to show them to Judith Marriner. Why would he do that? Were some or all of the others known to Judith? Neighbours, people from hereabouts? Sailing friends of Jack Marriner's? If so, where was their boat?

It seemed to Pippa that these photographs had a message for her. They told her something she ought to know. She did not know what it was. They were pictures of intense banality — glamourless, middle-aged people having a conventional holiday in unfashionable seaside resorts. But somewhere in these garish, amateur prints there was a key.

Would the man with the knife mind her looking at the photographs?

It was difficult to believe in him.

Bunbury snuffled in his sleep under the kitchen table, and from the stove there was a comforting gurgle of the water boiling round the beans. It was warm and brightly lit; it had become familiar. It was safe and normal and ordinary. But in the room almost next door, the woman whose photographed face she was looking at had been knocked on the head and asphyxiated; and three or four miles away, in her own car, an unseen man had pricked the back of her neck with the point of a knife.

And in spite of these things, she was hungry.

'How did you come by these photographs, Miss Lees?' said the Detective Chief Superintendent.

'Um…' said Pippa. 'How did you come by them?'

'WPC Clegg found them on the kitchen table, when she was having her final look round at one o'clock this morning.'

'Oh.'

'Nobody went into the kitchen except you, from six-thirty in the evening until then.'

'Yes. Well. I didn't see any harm in looking at them. Photographs are meant to be looked at. That's why people take them.'

'The pictures include the deceased.'

'Yes.'

'Why did you not show them to us?'

'I'd only just found them, in a drawer.'

'You were searching through drawers?'

'I had to. For the scissors. They were in the wrong drawer. The photographs were on top of them. I can't think why. That was how I came on the photographs.'

'In a drawer in the kitchen.'

'Yes, that's what I'm telling you.'

'You had been living in the house for six days, cooking for yourself as well as feeding the dogs, and you had not inspected the kitchen drawers?'

'Well, not once I knew where everything was. You don't keep poking through drawers when you know the spoons are in a different one, and I knew where the scissors were, only they weren't, and I can't begin to imagine how they crept in under those photographs...'

The Detective Chief Superintendent was looking at her opaquely. He did not understand why she was telling such silly, transparent lies about the photographs.

'The photographs have been identified by Mr Michael Craik as the property of his late wife.'

'I thought they must be hers. Being pictures of her.'

'He has also identified the other subjects of the pictures.'

'Oh yes. Friends.'

'You know them?'

'No. I've never seen any of them. I wondered who they were. Just, um, innocent friends, I expect...'

Pippa waited for the Chief Superintendent to tell her who the ugly old people were. Of course he knew who they were, where they lived, what they did, what their relationship had been with Mary Craik, whether they might be inclined to murder her, and so forth. He had probably talked to them all, or had them talked to. He could easily and harmlessly satisfy Pippa's curiosity. But he was not going to do so.

'Friends,' he echoed in a neutral voice. 'Mr Craik tells me that some of the photographs are missing.'

'Oh. I don't know about that. You can tell if any prints are missing by looking at the negatives.'

'That had occurred to us, Miss Lees.'

'Well, yes, of course, so I should hope, you being detectives... If the negatives are there, you can have some more prints made.'

'That had also occurred to us. The negatives are not there.'

'Oh. Well. You can't have other prints made.'

'Somebody has abstracted four or five prints, remembered by Mr Craik, and the negatives from which they were made. The strips of negatives have been quite crudely cut. Most of them have been returned to the envelope in which they came from the laboratory.'

'Well, that was thoughtful. They can have more prints of the ones they've got, to make up for the ones they haven't got... I should think those negatives show fingerprints pretty well, don't they? I expect you thought of that.'

'It crossed our minds, Miss Lees. You will not be surprised to hear that there were no fingerprints on the negatives.'

'But I am surprised. Why shouldn't I be surprised? You don't think I wiped off the fingerprints, do you? I don't even know what the other pictures were pictures of. Were they quite different? Or the same? Because if they were the same, I can't see that there's really much loss...'

Pippa heard herself talking too much, as she had in previous interviews with this alarming man. She hoped it made her sound silly but innocent, but she was afraid she was sounding silly but guilty.

'It's time I did the hay-nets for the horses,' said Pippa.

The Chief Superintendent nodded. She scuttled out of the room.

But Dan Mallett had already filled and put out the hay-nets, hanging them well apart on the rails of the paddock so that the horses did not squabble over them.

CHAPTER 9

The wind swung, the sky silvered, the world whitened until a thin sun melted the frost. Pippa had to break the ice on the horses' buckets, even on the canaries' bath. The earth of the flower-beds was like concrete rubble, and the leaves of evergreen shrubs like ancient paper; the tall dead stems of dogwood under the apple trees were dusted with diamonds in the sunlight, so that they looked like Christmas decorations in a whimsical gift-shop.

The frost silenced all the birds which had been deluded into singing, except one robin near the house; his song was a feeble effort compared to his usual boastfulness.

Pippa threw handfuls of corn for the fantail pigeons as well as the bantams. She remembered that in doing so she was defying Judith Marriner.

What about Judith Marriner? Where on earth had she got to? Messages had gone out to Italy, to hotels and banks and airports. She was in somebody's villa, perhaps, on a remote Sicilian hillside, or in a cabin in the Ligurian Alps; or she had hopped across other seas to Turkey or Tunisia…

Perhaps she knew what had happened here, and she was staying away deliberately. That would not be a bad idea. She could do no good, and she would be maddened by meeting the police round every corner. Her coming back would not allow Pippa to leave.

It was strange that she had not rung up. That is to say, it would have been strange in anybody else. Anybody else would care about the dogs and horses.

Anybody else might even have worried about Pippa; but nobody in the world worried about Pippa except Mr Tomkins, the King Charles spaniel.

Pippa's Aunt Rosemary Gordon had formulated another law, as well as that concerned with reading-glasses lost in kitchen drawers. Her other law was about absent friends you suddenly thought of. If, shortly after you thought about them, the telephone rang, it was them. (Aunt Rosemary would have said, 'It was they,' but Pippa said, 'It was them.') It was not that they rang because you thought of them, Aunt Rosemary said, it was that you thought of them because they were going to ring.

As with kitchen scissors, she was right.

The telephone rang just before noon. Pippa took it in the hall; that telephone was on a table by the foot of the main stairs. She was now allowed to use the small sitting-room again, the body having been removed, all possible photographs taken, all fingerprinting completed, all other mysterious procedures gone through; she was allowed in there, but she did not want to go in there. She thought that only a ghoul could have used that room, talked on that telephone, sat in that chair.

She picked up the telephone in the hall, suddenly and illogically certain that the caller was Judith Marriner.

As she lifted the receiver, she heard a distant *ping*, which revealed that a policeman had lifted another extension, to listen in to the call.

There were buzzes and clicks, a faint throb of music like that of a juke-box at a distance, a curious fretted background of noise which might have been voices and the rattle of cutlery on plates, as though the caller were in a box in a passage outside a restaurant.

A female voice said, '*Avanti,*' and further rapid indecipherable words that sounded like Italian.

'Hallo?' shouted Pippa.

'Hallo? Hallo? Is that Philippa Lees? Is everything all right? I rang to say that I hope to be coming back —'

Click. Buzz. Electronic whinnying, as of an extra-terrestrial horse. Then the hum of a disconnected call, of a telephone ready for re-use.

Pippa rattled the knob of her telephone, knowing that it was stupid to do so. One always did, knowing it was stupid. People in films always did it, to show the audience that their telephone had been cut off.

Judith's voice had been distorted but recognizable. Why so distorted? Pippa had made calls to and from Italy, and their telephones were excellent. Was she much further away, but with Italians? In an Italian bar in Africa?

She had rung to say she was coming back, to say when she was coming. She wanted to be met at Heathrow, perhaps. She wanted food to be in the house, fires lit, preparations made, beds made up in other rooms; she wanted people to be told, messages delivered, calls made. She just wanted to make things easier for Pippa, saying when she was coming back so that Pippa could make plans? No, probably not. It was her own convenience she was concerned with. She had been spoiled by the old Hodges, and spoiled by life ever since, if you could call it being spoiled to have your husband drowning himself... Anyway, she wanted Pippa to know when she was coming back, and she would know she had been cut off, so she would ring again. All Pippa had to do was sit and wait for the call. The police would be sitting and waiting for it too, having heard everything that Pippa heard.

It was boring. The hall was large and draughty. Pippa became cold and uncomfortable, sitting in an upright chair by the telephone table. But she did not dare go far away from the telephone, since communication seemed to be so fragile.

The Sergeant who looked like a Hereford bullock came into the hall as though having nothing else to do. He stared at Pippa as she sat in the cold by the silent telephone, as her father's Hereford bullocks had stared at her over the fence of their field.

'No need for you to be tied to that phone, miss.'

'That was Mrs Marriner.'

'You recognized her voice?'

'Well, I think so. It was a rather bad line.'

'So our operator reported. But you know Mrs Marriner's voice and the WPC doesn't, so we depend on you to tell us if it really were the lady talkin'.'

'I think it was. She hardly had time to say anything. I'm sure she'll call again. I can't think why she hasn't called already, if she wanted me to know when she's coming.'

'Ar. Wants meetin', maybe. Likely call the garridge where they got her car.'

'Can you trace that call just now? Can you find out where she is?'

'Not comin' unexpected like that, wi' nobody alerted the other end, wi' all up an' over so quick, wi' no yuman element involved, so to say, all comin' by automatic exchanges. In the meantime, miss, don't feel obliged t'camp out here in the tundra just to be answerin' the phone. We'll take any message that'd come.'

'Oh. Well, thank you.'

'Go an' be cosy in the kitchen.'

The Sergeant was not her enemy, after all. The Detective Chief Superintendent was, but not the Sergeant. The Super had a sharp gingery face, like a fox. He had pale unfriendly eyes and a twitching nose. He was probably everybody's enemy; he was certainly Pippa's. He would not have been thoughtful like the Sergeant, seeing that she was cold and uncomfortable and bored, and taking pity on her.

Pippa put the dogs out. As she did so, she saw Dan Mallett by the stables, pumping up the back tyre of his bicycle. He looked out of place with the bicycle, incongruous, anachronistic. He belonged to an earlier age than that of bicycles. He should have travelled in a battered gig behind a shaggy pony.

At least, he should have when he was in the mode of the treacly, ludicrous rural voice. His other, educated voice went with a car better than Pippa's, with a Volvo or a Saab.

It was Mary Craik who had had the Volvo. Much good it had done her, in the end.

Glancing up from his bicycle pump, Dan saw Pippa. He stopped pumping, straightened and tugged off his disreputable cap. He smiled with what looked like friendly respect; he slightly bowed, not obsequiously but in greeting.

Pippa found that she had raised her hand to return his greeting; that she had even involuntarily smiled to return his smile; that she had done these things without meaning to or expecting to. She had forgotten for a moment her dark and vivid suspicions of this cocky little criminal, and also his insufferable presumption in kissing her.

As soon as she caught herself in the act, she lowered her hand and disciplined her face.

Dan Mallett finished his pumping. He took a spanner to the handle-bars of his bicycle. He began to take the bicycle to pieces.

Pippa remembered, with a sudden and destabilizing shock, the sensation of Dan Mallett's lips on hers, warm and dry and curiously friendly.

She remembered his voice, his other voice.

What was he about, after all? Who was he?

She did not think he had threatened her with a knife. It was still logically possible, but it had become somehow impossible. Absurdly, it was the texture of his lips that convinced her. They were not the lips of a man who threatened girls with knives.

Pippa knew where he lived. She could find the place again, obscurely tucked away though it was behind those tangly woods. She was consumed by curiosity.

The policeman had more or less told her to go away and amuse herself, to go wherever she wanted.

Dan Mallett was taking his bicycle to pieces. It looked like a job that would take him the rest of the day.

There might never be such a chance again.

Pippa put the dogs indoors and went across the yard to her car.

Pippa nosed the Renault along the bumpy track through the woods. She was suddenly aghast at what she was doing.

She was not aghast because she was snooping, although she was doing exactly that. She was not aghast because she risked enraging the man with the knife, although she was probably doing that too. She was aghast at what she might see, at the prospect of the reality of the cottage and the old mother.

One look, one sniff, would cure her for ever of being beguiled by those warm lips. Perhaps that was a good thing. A discriminating, snobbish, puritanical part of Pippa's mind said it was certainly a good thing.

Another part of her mind dreaded the truth about Dan Mallett.

And still she was consumed by curiosity.

She turned a corner by a dense clump of hazels, and there was the cottage in the midday sun.

It was not in the least as Pippa had expected — not as she had been told, not as she had imagined it, not as it had seemed in the dark.

It was still crazy, the roof too big and the windows too small, the uprights not vertical, the cross-pieces bent, bowed, and far from horizontal. But an upstairs window was open, showing bright checked curtains and a little room full of sunshine. The door also was open. The garden was tidy, with well-dug beds and a double row of Brussels sprouts and neatly pruned rose bushes. There were clothes on a line behind a clipped thorn hedge, shirts and underwear newly washed.

Between the car and the cottage was a large fenced pen, with grass and gravel and three kennels. There were the dogs she had heard. They were far from the mangy mongrels she had been led to expect. There was a big smooth-coated spotty dog, shining with health and muscled like a racehorse, which Pippa thought was a pointer. There was a sleek, disdainful, intensely elegant greyhound or lurcher, of a marvellous dark steel-grey. Making the most noise — a sort of Jacob in this haughty company — was a busy, obtrusive, exhibitionist Jack Russell terrier.

All the dogs were guarding their kingdom — Dan Mallett's kingdom — against the invader. They were well-fed and well-groomed. They had a big stone bowl of clean water, and the Jack Russell had a rubber bone as big as himself.

A figure appeared at the door of the cottage, evidently brought by the noise of the dogs. It was an old lady, stooped, walking stiffly and with difficulty. She was a very neat old lady, with black woollen stockings and a shawl and a cameo brooch, and white hair tightly gathered into a bun at the back of her head; an old lady with a face so white and wrinkled that it resembled crumpled tissue-paper, and red mittens, and bright blue eyes, memorable eyes.

They were Dan Mallett's eyes.

She was Dan Mallett's mother.

What in heaven's name had Judith Marriner been talking about?

The old lady called to the dogs, to quieten them. The pointer and the lurcher fell obediently silent, but the Jack Russell continued to yap, wagging his stump of a tail, showing off and enjoying himself.

The old lady looked at Pippa, waiting for her to get out of the car and explain herself. She was not hostile: she was simply waiting to be told who Pippa was and what she wanted. Her eye was bright with intelligence. She would stand no nonsense. She would be difficult to fool for a minute, and impossible to fool for long. Pippa's reason for bothering her would have to be a good one.

Pippa felt a fool. She should have been prepared, and she was not. She had not foreseen having to justify herself. She had nothing ready to say or do. She felt impertinent and gauche.

She got out of the car and walked up the cinder garden path to the door. She felt she was walking self-consciously, awkwardly, under the scrutiny of that bright old eye. The Jack Russell kept her company, dancing along inside the netting of the pen.

'I was looking for Dan Mallett,' said Pippa, when the moment arrived at which she had to say something.

'Dan ben up Marriner's,' said the old lady. 'As well ye know.'

Pippa gave a sort of hiccup of surprise.

'Ye ben the young lady looken after they dogs an' all, 'at Muz Marriner found a-Lunnon.'

'Well, yes.'

'So ye seen Dan up 'ere 'smornen, tinkeren wi' 'at ol' bike.'

'Well, yes.'

'Ye had a mind t'see where Dan bides. So be. 'Tes normal. 'Ere's been a score o' maids cam' for t'be pryen an' prodden.'

A score of girls had come to inspect Dan's cottage and his mother and his lifestyle — girls who had seen his remarkable blue eyes, girls full of curiosity, silly snooping childish girls whom Dan had hooked and whom he was playing like trout...

And Pippa was one of them, just another undignified little nosy chit. It was not Dan or his mother who had put Pippa into this shaming category — it was Pippa who had put herself there.

'How did you know I was at Mrs Marriner's?' said Pippa, to get away from the subject of why she was visiting Dan's.

'Dan said t'me ye'd come. He said how ye did look.'

'What did he say?' asked Pippa, before she could stop herself.

The old lady looked at her blankly, as though she had not heard. Pippa was reproved. She was being silently twitted for being vulgar and undignified. She was being given a sharp lesson in deportment by an old peasant who lived in a crazy cottage under a dripping wood.

'Ye've seen the palace,' said the old lady, and turned to go back into the cottage.

Pippa was dismissed.

When she drove away, the barking of the Jack Russell sounded like derisive laughter.

Mary Craik had had the Volvo, and now Michael Craik had it. Pippa saw it in the village, in Medwell Zelston, pulling away from the newsagent's.

Michael Craik looked quite at home at the wheel of the powerful, heavy car.

'I said to Mr Lewis,' said Pippa's friend with the coconut matting hair, 'look at us, how honoured we are, I said, the aristocracy descending on our humble emporium like locusts.'

'You didn't say nothing o' the sort,' said Mr Lewis miserably.

'Not word for word, I grant you. I'm givin' the gist.'

'What you said was a load o' snail-trail.'

'Elegant criticism I call that. He do use the rapier, don't he, rather than the bludgeon? It's an education, sittin' at his feet. Talkin' o' feet, that Mr Michael Craik gets a lovely polish on 'is shoes. Kiwi, would that be? Meltonian Cream? Wi' a drop o' champagne? Pink champagne they used on their hunting boots in the good old days. Made them good enough to eat, I daresay. Hence the phrase "Lickin' their boots".'

'Stop jestin' do,' said Mr Lewis. 'Goes through me like a skewer.'

'Laughter makes the world go round,' said the woman. 'That an' money. Mr Michael Craik would agree with that. He loves a laugh. He wouldn't know about money so much, 'cos he never had any. It's strange to glimpse 'im drivin' a luxurious limousine. I should think 'e 'ardly knows 'isself. "Who's that?" he cries. "Blimey, it's me."'

'Do belt up. Do put a sock in it.'

'Poor Mrs Craik's that was, that snarlin' roadster. She drove it all over, like tellin' everybody "Look at me!" It did come as a surprise, after the little old Escort she 'ad. Tradin' up wi' a vengeance. Only the other day, too. She didn't 'ardly live to enjoy 'er status symbol. I call that a tragic irony. Mr Lewis does, too. 'E might not admit it to everybody, but in 'is 'eart of 'earts 'e calls it a tragic irony.'

It struck Pippa that, gabby as the woman was, what she said was true. The big shiny Volvo was indeed a status symbol, and the status was far higher than the gimcrack house in the scrubby little garden where Mary Craik had lived. It was an entirely improbable car for her to have had. With it she had replaced a small old Ford. That was the car that went with Berryes. How had she suddenly found all those thousands of pounds?

Her own thousands? Had Michael left her any? If he had, why hadn't she used them before, if big cars were what she liked?

'She suddenly went out and bought it?' said Pippa, thinking aloud rather than asking a question.

'Well, it wasn't a present, dear, was it, pardon the liberty of so addressin' a member of the gentry. Yuss, Father Christmas put fifteen thousand Bradburies under her pillow, an' off she went hoppity-hop to the showroom. She come back zoom-zoom, proud as a peacock, makin' excuses to drive hither an' yon, by way of drawin' attention. Poor Mr Michael, he were never allowed be'ind the wheel. 'E 'ad to be content wi' 'is old ancient banger, bang, clang, the exhaust-pipe falls off 'ere, the 'eadlights falls off there, the County Council comes pantin' along be'ind wi' a special van, pickin' up the bits o' that car.'

'You're gettin' fanciful,' said Mr Lewis. 'You're drivellin'.'

'A touch o' the poetics. Paintin' in bold colours. Some 'as souls an' some not.'

'When did Mrs Craik buy the Volvo?' asked Pippa, not knowing why she wanted to know.

'Ow!' said Mr Lewis. 'October.'

'November,' said the woman.

'In the autumn,' said Pippa quickly.

Mr Lewis and the woman glanced at one another in triumph, as though each had been proved right.

'When was it she went on holiday in France?' asked Pippa, sure that these two would know.

'August,' said Mr Lewis.

'September,' said the woman.

'This las' year jus' been,' said Mr Lewis.

Pippa expected the woman to say that it had been the year before, but she was silent. She accepted that the car had been bought, the holiday taken, in the later months of the previous year.

Could it be cause and effect? How could it? Why should it? Pippa did not know why she had asked about the holiday immediately after talking about the expensive new car.

Had Michael Craik killed his wife because she went away on holiday with another man?

Had he killed her in order to drive her smart new Volvo?

How had he killed her, if he had been in the pub all evening? With somebody's help? With Dan Mallett's help?

They found the other photographs, the ones missing from the set of holiday snapshots. Shamelessly eavesdropping, Pippa heard a detective telling a policewoman about it. They had been once again searching Berryes, looking for things they had not previously known they should have been looking for. These photographs were precisely such things. They were found in a drawer in a desk. They might have been seen in an earlier search, without any significance being attached to them. Presumably they had been there, in that drawer in that desk, but it was impossible to be sure. Mr Craik identified them, but anybody could have told that they belonged with the others.

'What was special about them?' asked the policewoman.

'Nothing wasn't special about them,' said the detective. 'They was no more nor less than the others. Same sort o' places, same people. Maybe some other people, but too far off to identify.'

'Magnified?'

'They tried in the lab, blowin' up the negatives on a screen. Jus' blobby blurs. Amateur snaps, o' course. These other faces was passers-by, like, in the distance, not properly intended as targets, so to say.'

Pippa was in the downstairs cloakroom, in the dark because the bulb had popped. She did not know where Judith Marriner kept spare bulbs. It was a thing they had not discussed, that they had forgotten about. The door of the cloakroom was ajar. The detective and the policewoman were just inside the back door. Pippa supposed that she should show herself, interrupt, make her presence known, before anything confidential was said. Nothing had been, yet. None of this stuff about photographs meant anything at all.

Pippa decided she did not need to feel guilty about eavesdropping, because they had been eavesdropping on her. They had listened in when Judith Marriner had rung up. They would listen to anything anybody said to her, including a lover, if she had one of those. That made it fair for her to listen.

'Mr Craik, 'e says there's still one missin',' said the detective.

'One photo? One of that lot?'

'So Mr Craik says.'

'What's it of?'

"E don't know. Can't remember it special.'

'If he can't remember it, how does he know it's not there?'

'Numberin'. 'E says 'e remembers distinct there was forty-eight photographs. It was amazin', because every single shot came out. Never 'appened before, 'e says.'

'That never happened to me, neither. There's always one or two blurred, or a thumb in front of the lens.'

'Same wi' us. Same wi' everybody, in the ordinary way. It's a thing you would remember, forty-eight photos, an' every single one comes out. Well, you might remember or not, but 'e does.'

'It mus' be so. He wouldn't say that if it wasn't so. Nobody wouldn't invent a stupid thing like that.'

'Yes, right. Well, now there's only the forty-seven, prints an' negatives both an' all matchin'. Definitely there's one gone shy.'

'But we don't know what of.'

'No, 'cept it's same like the rest.'

'Then what's the hassle?'

'I dunno,' said the detective. 'I dunno if there is any hassle.'

The wind had swung again, to the west and the south-west, and a soft rain was followed by watery sunshine, a day like April, a day when a boot in the rough grass seemed certain to squash an upthrusting daffodil.

Pippa took one of the polythene panels off the side of the aviary, so that the warm fresh air visited the little yellow birds. It made them, too, suddenly and gloriously certain that spring had arrived.

Pippa knew that only the cocks sang. She thought there were eight or nine cocks. Some were almost white, some with a flush of apricot, two with sketchy blackish skull-caps. All these small gentlemen found perches high off the ground, and began to warble and trill, in greeting to the pale sun, in competition with one another. Pippa watched and listened, transfixed. The singing was beautiful. The voices blended into a magic choir, a sound beyond music, a sound of angels. It was amazing that these tiny creatures could produce such strong and lovely shouts. They expanded their chests; they vibrated with the passion of their singing.

Pippa had come indoors, into the kitchen and the brick-floored utility room next to the kitchen; it was from this room that the glass door opened into the porch where the aviary had been made. Looking through the glass into the aviary, Pippa could see through the wire mesh into the garden. She could see that someone was standing on the gravel path which ran past the porch and round the corner of the house. It was a big man in a husky waistcoat over a tweed jacket. He was standing stock still, attentive, listening with almost painful concentration to the singing of the birds. He was staring at the birds so fixedly that he did not notice Pippa beyond the glass of the door, although she must have been plainly visible to him.

He loved the birds. His face showed that he was almost intolerably moved by their music.

It was strange to see him there. He was not a man in whom you would have guessed there would be such soft feeling, such strong emotion.

It was Michael Craik.

The love in his face was real. He must have been aware of it, but unaware of showing it. He was not putting it on for anybody, because he did not know that he was being watched. Pippa was embarrassed, because he was baring his soul.

His love of Parsonage Farm, of the way of life of this house, was not altogether envy, emulation, greedy snobbery. Under the coarse features and the high gloss there was somewhere concealed a kind of poetry.

Pippa thought Michael Craik's soul was not a very big one. She thought her own was pretty small, too. She thought Mary Craik's had been even smaller, and Judith Marriner did not have one at all.

Did Dan Mallett have a soul? He had kissed her. Did that suggest that he had a soul, or that he hadn't?

The man with the knife was the prowler in the dark, and the voice on the telephone. He said he was the shadow on the ceiling. He was the murderer. He would murder again. He would murder Pippa if she found out anything about him. He said so, and Pippa believed him, because she had felt the point of his knife.

Then why on earth had he advertised himself, with his voice on the telephone, with his footstep on the gravel? Why had he taken the crazy risk of hiding in the back of her car? Was he showing off, proving how clever he was? There were criminals who did that, clever-clever psychopaths mocking the police with telephone calls and postcards and false clues, thinking themselves Robin Hoods or matadors or Harlequins, dancing into the spotlight, dancing out of reach...

Dancing. The word rang a bell.

Who had been dancing, too clever by half? Who had been talking, and about whom? An elusive memory mocked Pippa from the shadowy edge of her brain, flickering out of reach, out of sight, when she tried to grab it, as deceptive, perhaps as dangerous, as the dancer someone had been talking about...

CHAPTER 10

From the window of the downstairs cloakroom Pippa saw that the light was on in the tack-room.

Dan Mallett was doing her work for her again.

Pippa had expected to be rendered immune to Dan Mallett by seeing the squalor in which he lived. It had not worked out like that.

If Judith Marriner was so grossly wrong about Dan's mother, was she equally wrong about Dan himself?

Pippa was suddenly, urgently anxious to ask Dan Mallett whether he had ever actually been to prison. She hurried along the passage and out of the back door, passing the uniformed constable who was on duty there.

'I'm needed in the stable,' she said over her shoulder.

The policeman raised and lowered his eyebrows. He probably knew that she was not needed in the stable at all.

As Pippa emerged into the darkness of the yard, an unfamiliar car nosed into it. It was similar to Pippa's mother's car, but older and more battered, a grey Renault 5 with dents in the wings. Out of it climbed a woman in jeans and a big woolly sweater, wearing a man's tweed cap. In the gathering dusk, Pippa saw a blink of very fair hair, cut short, under the green checked cap. It was Dan Mallett's girl, the needlessly lovely girl who had gone off with Mrs Marriner's expensive hunting saddle.

The girl opened the back of her car and pulled out the saddle. She put it over her arm and carried it into the stable. Evidently she was not a thief. But she was up to no good.

Pippa had been engaged precisely to protect this place against such people.

Pippa paused outside the tack-room door, which was ajar. The questions she wanted to ask Dan Mallett could not be asked in front of a stranger. She hovered uncertainly. She had the feeling that, from the house, she would look as though she was lurking and eavesdropping, spying, snooping. She thought the smooth-voiced man with the knife would think she was doing those things, but wherever he was, whoever he was, he was definitely not in the house.

He might be in the tack-room, though. He might be the man getting the horses' feeds together. This was still objectively possible. Logically, a man could have a neat, intensely respectable mother, and also have a big sharp knife. It was hard to believe that the business of the knife had happened, that smarmy terrifying voice coming out of the dark, inches behind her, and the point of the knife pricking the nape of her neck.

'I found out something you might be interested in,' said the girl's clear, expensive, irritating voice.

'Anything you tell me is interesting,' said the voice which was, incredibly, Dan Mallett's.

'About Michael Craik in the pub, the night his wife was murdered.'

'Are you going to tell me he was there, or that he wasn't there?'

'Do you know a man called Albert Godden?'

'Curly Godden? Tolerably well. If you have any gold teeth, keep your mouth shut when Curly's anywhere near.'

'That's what everybody says about you, darling.'

The girl's use of the endearment made Pippa feel ashamed to be listening, but not so ashamed that she stopped doing so.

Dan Mallett made a noise that sounded like a chuckle. There was another noise that might have been a kiss. Pippa thought it was only a friendly kiss, but she did not know why she thought so.

'Curly Godden,' said Dan, 'hasn't told the truth, except by mistake, more than once a week in the last sixty years.'

'Then probably you don't want to hear what he said about Michael Craik in the pub.'

'You're bent on telling me,' said Dan. 'Nothing I can do will stop you.'

'Oh, you horrible little man,' said the girl, with deep affection. 'Albert Godden said they were all amazed that Mr Craik spent so long in the Chestnut Horse. He doesn't usually hob-nob with the village.'

'That thought has occurred to everybody.'

'There was a reason he was there, that he was showing himself.'

'He was giving himself an alibi?'

'That's what they all think. Because he wanted Judith Marriner. He wanted this house. So he'd be suspected. So he sat in the pub all evening. That's what they all think.'

'He knew it was going to happen? He'd hired himself a hitman from Milchester? Is that how the best brains in the village have worked it out?'

'Not quite. Mr Godden says Michael Craik went off to the loo. He was gone a long time. But he definitely didn't go off in his car. His old car makes a frightful noise, apparently, which was the one he used until he inherited his new one.'

'All perfectly true. All lending credence to what follows, I hope.'

'You talk far, far too much. Michael Craik couldn't possibly have walked all the way out here and killed her and gone back again, not in the time he was out, even though it was a long time for going to the loo.'

'Curly made an accurate note of the time Michael Craik took to have a slash in the Gents' behind the pub? I don't believe it.'

'No, of course not. He just remembers that Michael Craik was a long time going to the loo, because it made him wonder if Michael Craik was being sick, or had an upset tummy, or something.'

'And that would make Curly wonder if he could safely nick something out of Michael Craik's car.'

'Do shut up. He was a long time going to the loo, but not long enough to walk out here from the middle of the village, and he definitely didn't go anywhere in a car. But…'

'Are we coming to the interesting part? You do keep a chap on tenterhooks.'

'Suddenly today Mr Godden remembered about his bicycle.'

'Whose bicycle?'

'His. Albert Godden's.'

'I bet he pinched it.'

'As a matter of fact, he did. That's why he hasn't mentioned it to the police.'

'Mentioned what? I still don't know what we're talking about.'

'That's because you keep interrupting. Albert Godden says he left his bicycle in one place when he went into the pub, and found it in a different place when he came out.'

'Are we sure Curly wasn't drunk?'

'I don't know. Does he get drunk?'

'No. Head like a traffic bollard, and also too mean. Is the scenario that Michael Craik went off to the Gents', borrowed Curly Godden's bike, sped up here, coaxed his wife into that little room with the telephone…'

'He didn't have to. He rang up.'

'Curly hasn't got a mobile phone on his bike.'

'He used the telephone in the annexe, Lady What's-her-name's telephone.'

'Are we assuming he had a key to the annexe?'

'Of course he did, if he wanted one. He had anything here he wanted. He was having an affair with Judith Marriner.'

'Hmm,' said Dan.

'He's a very fit, powerful man, not a weedy little runt like you. He could whizz up here on a bicycle in no time, let himself into the annexe, ring up, that gets her to the telephone, he lets himself into the main house, she's sitting by the telephone, bonk.'

'Bonk doesn't mean what it used to mean.'

'All right, bang.'

'Bang doesn't, either.'

'*Will you shut up?*'

'Did Curly Godden tell you this about his bike?'

'He was thinking aloud. He was outside the post office. He suddenly bashed his forehead with his hand. He said, "Some bastard must've borrowed my bike."'

'Ah,' said Dan. 'Yes, he would be struck by that. He never uses that bike by day, only in the comforting shroud of darkness, when nobody can see that it's one he borrowed and hung on to. Somebody borrowing it from him could be deeply embarrassing for Curly. I do see his point. So he launched into a soliloquy?'

'He sort of muttered for a bit, but I heard it all quite clearly. What I've been telling you. Then he saw me listening. He scowled at me and bolted away like a rabbit.'

'Ah,' said Dan, 'well, now. The large, slow gentlemen in blue are perfectly convinced there was *no* bicycle outside the

Chestnut Horse that night. Curly didn't tell them about his, naturally, and nobody else had seen it. Well, well. Everybody's theory now becomes objectively possible. He kidnapped the little dog much earlier, which is a thing very few people could have done, he wired it to the gatepost, having stashed it meanwhile I'm not sure where, all this with object of getting little Pippa out of the way...'

Pippa was furious at this patronizing reference. She stood still and stayed quiet.

'Speaking of whom,' said Dan, raising his voice, 'aren't you getting cold out there, Miss Lees?'

'No,' said Pippa, without thinking.

'The only thing wrong with your theory, Libby, is that it's wrong.'

'You said that before, the last time I came here.'

'Probably. I keep nothing from you. Saddle, theories, everything that's mine is yours.'

There was silence. Pippa stood thinking. The girl in the tack-room was no doubt thinking.

Pippa thought: she was called Libby something. An American diminutive, though the girl was not American. How was she involved with Dan Mallett, and why was her theory wrong?

This Libby creature might be a tart and a snooper and a borrower of saddles, but her idea about the murder was obviously right.

Pippa felt silly, caught eavesdropping. She could not imagine how Dan Mallett had known she was there. She was cold.

There was a relaxed intimacy in the way that those two talked to one another, cosy in the tack-room, which Pippa dimly remembered from another life, from her life with Fenton Row...

She forbade her mind to finish saying the name. She had not thought of him for hours, what with expeditions to Dan Mallett's cottage. She refused to think of him now.

There were noises of farewell from the tack-room, sickeningly affectionate. The Libby creature came out. She did not see Pippa. Probably she thought Pippa had gone away.

Pippa went into the tack-room, bursting with questions.

She wanted to say, 'Why don't you think Michael Craik killed his wife?'

She wanted to say, 'Have you ever been to prison?'

She said, 'How did you know I was going to your cottage?'

'Because it's exactly what I would have done, if I'd been you,' said Dan Mallett mildly, in his educated voice.

'Why?'

'Local opinion will have given you a jaundiced view of my morals and behaviour, which could have led you to suppose that I might have been an accessory to that murder, if not the murderer. All kinds of things would lend weight to such a notion, including my ancient friendship with little Jacob. So, in courageous pursuit of the truth, you felt obliged to do some research into my background.'

'Hmm,' said Pippa, not much satisfied with this. She wanted to ask how Dan had described her to his mother. She just stopped herself. She said instead, 'You must know your girlfriend's theory is right.'

'Mine is more elegant.'

'Judith Marriner said you were constantly in and out of prison.'

'It's a widely held view, but exaggerated. I should languish in prison. Besides, my mother would die of rage if I wasn't there to cook her breakfast.'

'You've *never* been in jug?'

'Some say by luck, some by magic. The Super thinks I evade arrest by dint of witchcraft.'

'You could have caught Jake, and taken him away, and then tied him to that gatepost when you knew Michael Craik was ready, to get me out of the house. You could have done that better than anybody else in the world.'

'I'm not certain if that's a compliment. Why would I assist a nasty man to do such a nasty thing?'

'Because he had a hold over you. He caught you stealing something. So you had to tie up little dogs if he told you to. Possibly you did much more than that. Are you sure you've never been to prison?'

'I do believe I'd remember, if I had. I don't think it's a thing one would forget.'

'I can't understand about your voice.'

'Simple fun, really. It amuses my various employers.'

'It disarms them, so you get away with murder.'

'I hope you mean that figuratively.'

Pippa was silent for a moment, thinking with amazement of the Dan Mallett she had first met using the word 'figuratively'.

'Well, never mind for the moment about what you did,' said Pippa, considerably surprising herself. 'You know Michael Craik wanted Judith Marriner and her money and this house and the stable and paddocks and horses and dogs and canaries and bantams, and even those shelves and shelves of awful Victorian novels, and all those dreary little watercolours in dingy gilt frames...'

'Yes,' said Dan Mallett. 'But Michael could have had all those things without killing the poor woman. Everybody gets divorced all the time. It's shocking to an old moralist like me. Even if Mary Craik had been a passionate Papist, she couldn't have kept Michael on a string, not for ever, not if he could afford to leave her. And if he went to Judith he could afford it.'

'Well then,' said Pippa, becoming used to the extraordinary sensation of having this extraordinary conversation, 'why didn't Michael Craik just walk out on his wife? Did she have a hold over him? Could she have had him sent to prison for something? Did she have brothers he was frightened of? If he could get a divorce, why didn't he get one? Did she have much more money than anybody knew about?'

'Not until recently,' said Dan.

'Recently. She bought that Volvo recently.'

'Somebody bought it.'

'She suddenly had a lot of money, so Michael killed her for it.'

'No, love.'

'What did you call me? What did you say to your mother about me?'

'Enough so she'd recognize you when you came.'

'The spot on my nose, or my big feet?'

'A-ben sayen,' said Dan, in a voice suddenly of dark treacle, ''at ye been the most beauteous maidie ever been spied o' thicky part. 'At were enough fur m'mam to know 'ee.'

Pippa burst out laughing. It was not only amusement at his performance, the cunning of his disarming leprechaun act: it was also the huge relief of believing him. He had never been in prison or anywhere near prison. He was the son of an intensely respectable old lady, to whom he was a dutiful and devoted son. All the calumny spread about him, by Judith Marriner and Mr Lewis in the newsagent's and the rest, was probably derived from the threat of those amazing blue eyes.

They were a threat, indeed.

Dan smiled at her laughter. He kissed her, and disappeared out of the tack-room and away in the darkness.

Pippa found that her knees were wobbling. She sat down on the corn-bin.

It was not only those blue eyes, not only that ridiculous virtuoso performance. Also Dan was clever.

He was too clever. He had a theory about the murder which he described as 'elegant'. He was treating the whole thing as a game, a charade, the most artistic solution being the winner.

It was true, Pippa acknowledged, that Michael Craik was an altogether boring suspect, the most obvious of all possible culprits. But this news about the bicycle, destroying his alibi, put the question beyond doubt.

It was boring and obvious that he had done it: it was boringly and obviously true.

Why did he have to murder her?

Presumably the police could puzzle out the motives, which presumably had to do with money, property, inheritance, capital transfer tax, clauses in wills, and infinitely dreary matters such as these. Probably the police already knew all about all of that, because it would all be sitting in deed-boxes in lawyers' offices. The police knew Michael Craik had done it, but they had come up against his alibi in the pub.

Ha.

Who knew about the bicycle? Michael Craik did, but he wasn't going to tell about it. Old Curly Godden knew about it, but he wasn't going to tell. Dan knew, but he wasn't going to spoil the elegance of his own solution. The creature Libby knew, but she wasn't going to tell because Dan didn't want her to, and she was putty in Dan's hands. Pippa was not putty in anybody's hands. She was tough, hardened by experience, blue eyes and comic rural monologues notwithstanding. Her public duty had not always been clear to her, but this time it was.

The police would go away, and peace would descend.

Pippa locked up the tack-room and went to make the statement that would end the story.

'How do you come to know about this bicycle, Miss Lees?' said the Detective Chief Superintendent.

'I heard a girl called Libby telling somebody about it.'

'Telling whom?'

'Well, it was Dan Mallett.'

'I see. You heard a girl telling Dan Mallett.'

'Well, it can still be true, even if it was told to Dan Mallett.'

'A girl called Libby. May we know more about this person?'

'Um, she has fair hair.'

'You know her name?'

'Libby.'

'No more?'

'Um, no. I mean, I've forgotten.'

'You saw them together, when she was giving this information to Mallett?'

'Um, no. I couldn't actually see them.'

'You know the girl well, even though you do not know her name?'

'Um, no.'

'You have at least met her?'

'No.'

'Yet you confidently and positively identify her voice?'

'Well, yes, because...'

'She was at the Chestnut Horse on the evening in question?'

'Um, no, not as far as I know.'

'But she said in your hearing that Godden left his bicycle outside the Chestnut Horse all that time?'

'Yes.'

'How did she know?'

'Mr Godden told her. She saw him in the street.'

'She said that Godden told her about his bicycle?'

'Um, no, he was talking to himself.'

'I see.'

'Ask Dan Mallett.'

'Ask him what, Miss Lees?'

'Whether this is true!'

'I am to ask Dan Mallett if Curly Godden was talking to himself in the village street? Dan Mallett was not there. How should he know?'

'He was told.'

'And now we have been told. Thank you.'

'Well, none of them would ever have told you! Obviously none of them ever would.'

'I am confused, Miss Lees. None of whom would ever have told us what?'

'About the bicycle. Not Michael Craik, or Godden, or Dan Mallett, or that Libby person…'

'Dan Mallett might not have told us that a bicycle he did not see was outside a public house he did not visit, is that what Dan Mallett would not have told us? Might he also not have told us that the President of the United States only ate half his helping of asparagus that evening? He could easily not tell us that. In fact, I believe he has not told us that.'

'Asparagus,' said Pippa stupidly. 'What has asparagus to do with it?'

'Comparatively, it is a miracle of relevance,' said the Detective Chief Superintendent.

'Those photographs,' said Pippa to Dan in the morning, over Talisman's back in the loosebox. 'One of the Craiks must have brought them across for Judith Marriner to see. Because she knew the other people.'

'Something like that. They only brought some. An edited selection.'

'Yes, because the others were even more boring. But one was completely missing, still is, print and negative both.'

'Mary Craik abstracted it, print and negative both.'

'Yes. Why did she?'

'A picture she wanted to hide. A secret she wanted to keep.'

'A man,' said Pippa. 'She had a boyfriend in France. She was meeting him that night, that awful night. Yes, yes! She was excited. She was a bit drunk, I think, but she was … avid.'

'Imagination boggles,' said Dan.

'I know. It shouldn't, but it does. She was meeting a man she couldn't meet at home, and she couldn't have met him at Judith's if Judith hadn't been away, but it didn't matter me seeing him, because I didn't know any of them… Yes. I bet anything you like she was meeting the man in that missing photograph.'

'Unless there were a lot of men in her life, I think that must be right.'

'Do you think there were a lot of men in her life? *Could* there have been?'

'Let us not speak ill of the dead,' said Dan unctuously, 'but I doubt if Mary Craik was wildly pursued or hectically promiscuous.'

'Unlike some,' said Pippa.

'Leave we not speak ill o' th' liven, neither,' said Dan, in a voice of slow molasses.

Once again Pippa laughed at the sudden switch of voices, and once again Dan kissed her as he departed, before she could do or say anything.

If Dan Mallett was too clever, the police were too stupid. They were utterly stupid not to accept the evidence about the bicycle.

It was funny that Dan Mallett and the police refused to believe the obvious truth, but for opposite reasons.

It was the obvious truth if the Libby person had got it right. It hung on the actual character of old Godden. Pippa had only heard Dan's account of that. She was not sure he was a reliable source.

She needed a cross-bearing, and after her days in the neighbourhood she knew exactly where to get it.

'Curly Godden,' said Mr Lewis miserably, in the little overcrowded newsagent's shop. 'Ow. Stickiest fingers in fifty parishes, always exceptin' that Dan Mallett.'

'There 'e goes again,' said the woman with coconut-matting hair. 'Always coinin' the happy phrase. Quite startlin' sometimes, the original things he do come up with.'

'I heard about a bicycle,' said Pippa, in a terribly casual way.

'We didn't hear about no cycle, did we, Mr Lewis? We heard about sundry items from the supermarket down Milchester. Scented soaps, for to beautify the person.'

'Ow,' said Mr Lewis. 'If 'e tries that in 'ere, I'll cut 'is 'and off wi' me bill — 'ook.'

'More the harsh attitude to punishment, 'as Mr Lewis,' said the woman. 'An eye for an eye an' a tooth for a tooth, supposin' 'e retained any o' them amongst the porcelain dentures.'

'An' I'd cut the tongues out o' gabby old bags,' said Mr Lewis.

'The delicacy of 'is wit is something to treasure, same like a dancin' sunbeam.'

It was credible, then, the oddity of a stolen bicycle used only at night. It was all true and the police *were* absolutely stupid.

'Dancing sunbeam.' Dancing shadows, dancing feet, something like that had come up.

Could a man who listened entranced to the music of songbirds be the same man who knocked out his wife with a poker and then asphyxiated her with a cushion over her face? Could two such people exist inside one skin?

He wanted the canaries so badly for his own that he killed to get them? Was that possible?

Pippa had got into the way of checking up on the horses, last thing before she went to bed. It went with putting the dogs out for their last run. It was what they had done in her parents' house. It was what almost everybody did who had horses and dogs. It was saying goodnight to the horses, having a final word with them — it was almost more that than checking their bedding, hay, water, stable-rugs. Pippa knew that there was no need to check anything, since Dan Mallett had put the horses to bed. He would have seen to everything, for some reason doing her job for her. But though there was no need to check, she would always do it. Nearly all people with horses would do it.

Anybody who had been watching her would know that she would look in on the horses before she went to bed, while the dogs trotted out onto the lawn.

That was how it was. Somebody had been watching her, and he knew her routine. He knew that if he waited quietly in the dark in the stables, she would walk into his trap.

He knew that it would not be very late. She had nothing to stay up late for. He would not be kept waiting long. Of course he knew that. From the stable he could see the upstairs windows of the house. He could see if the lights were on in the upstairs passage. If they went on and then went off, he would know that she had gone to bed without calling in on the horses. Then he would simply leave it until the next night.

In the event, he did not have to wait and he did not have to postpone it. Pippa behaved as normal, which was very nearly the end of her. It all went exactly according to plan, his plan.

At eleven-twenty, Pippa put the dogs out. Old Bunbury did not want to go, but in the end she persuaded him to follow the others onto the grass. She crossed the yard to the stables. She opened the door onto the dense darkness inside. One of the horses moved a foot, gently rustling the straw of its bedding. A bantam chuckled sleepily from the loft. Pippa stepped over the threshold and reached for the light-switch.

A scarf or some broad strip of coarse material went round her head from behind, covering the lower half of her face, pulled tight immediately, gagging her, stopping her from breathing, pulling her backwards off balance so that she could not turn and struggle. Her arms were grabbed and pulled behind her back and held painfully. She felt something hard in the small of her back, a knee or a chunk of wood. She was held by somebody much stronger than she was. She struggled, but all she did was hurt herself. She panicked, because she could not breathe. Panic made her struggle uselessly, and the effort of struggling made her desperate for air.

'I did ask you not to snoop,' said a voice behind her.

It was the voice she knew. It was the false voice, the muffled and disguised voice of the midnight telephone; it was the voice of the man in the back of the car, with the big sharp knife.

'Now look what you've got yourself into,' said the voice. 'Much the worst trouble you've ever been in in your life.'

CHAPTER 11

Pippa gave a desperate moan through her gag, begging for breath. It seemed he understood. He pulled the gag downwards, so that it was just clear of Pippa's nostrils, while still painfully strapping her mouth. She could make a kind of moaning noise, a cow-like inhuman helpless bellowing noise, but it was not very loud. It would hardly be heard from the house. It would not sound strange, coming from the stables, even if anybody heard it.

'Shut up,' said the man, twisting her arm behind her back.

She heard herself give a muffled whinny of pain. But she was doing no good by making any noise she could make, and it caused him to hurt her, so she stopped.

She thought it was impossible that she should not recognize the voice. But she did not recognize it. It might have been Michael Craik's or it might not. It might have been Dan Mallett's voice — one of his voices — or it might not. It might have been somebody she knew or somebody she did not know.

Pippa whimpered from the pain of her arms twisted behind her back and the rough gag twisted over her mouth.

She did not know why this was happening. She had not really been prying. She had asked one or two questions to which everybody in the neighbourhood knew the answers; she had overheard one or two conversations; anything she had told the police they either knew already or else did not believe. There was a misunderstanding. This vicious bully behind her thought she knew something she didn't. She would have said this if she could have said anything, but the only noise she could make was the complaint of an old, sick animal.

'You and your photographs,' said the smooth, false voice.

Photographs. There was one batch, and another batch not much different, and one missing.

What was special about that one? Why had Mary Craik removed it, if she had?

Pippa's mind was not working well, because she was cold and very frightened, and her arms and mouth were hurting. But she thought she saw that the missing photograph was the reason for all this.

She tried to say she had never seen it, but she could only mumble and whimper against the gag.

The horses rustled the straw round their feet. They sniffed and sighed and mumbled their crumbs in their mangers. They were unaware of knives and terror.

Probably the dogs had gone in. Probably they were settled in their various places, not giving thought to any human problem.

'I don't think you've shown it to anybody yet,' said the voice, 'and I don't think you're going to show anything to anybody, ever again.'

Pippa tried to say, 'I haven't got it, I've never seen it,' but only a little animal mewing came out of the gag.

Suddenly, shockingly, there was pandemonium. There was a crash behind Pippa, the door crashing open against the back of the man who was holding her. There was a grunt from the man and a grunt from another man, two aggressive grunts, feet scraping on the cobblestones, blows, heavy breathing, swearing, more crashes. Something knocked Pippa over, into a corner of the stable, almost into the nearest loosebox. She was hurt on the hard floor. She found that her arms were free. She pulled off her gag. She was incapable at first of doing anything except panting and whimpering on the floor of the stable. In the pitch darkness there were heaves and bangs and scrapes and grunting and panting and minor crashes, two men fighting in pitch darkness. A bucket clanged away in the dark. There was a thud at ground level, a body falling into the angle of wall and floor.

There was a groan. A tall pale rectangle appeared, slightly less black than black, the door opening on to the yard. A figure silhouetted for a moment, black against not-quite-black, crouching, running. He ran away silently, maybe limping.

Pippa pulled herself to her feet, flapping her arms to bring them back to life. She was sobbing, from pain and fright and relief, and the pins-and-needles in her arms. She groped along the wall to the door and found the light-switch.

There was another groan from the floor at her feet. One of the men was still there. It was the man who attacked her or the man who attacked him. There was no knowing which it was.

Frightened of what she might see, Pippa turned on the light.

Dan Mallett was on his hands and knees at her feet, with blood all over his face Pippa screamed.

Speaking with evident difficulty, Dan Mallett said, 'A-ben sarry ye ban cruelled.'

'You don't have to talk like that to me.'

'Nor I do,' said Dan in his normal voice, if it was really his normal voice: something like his normal voice, as normal as it could be when he was panting harshly with exertion and pain.

Pippa sobbed once, from shock, from relief.

Talisman's big yellow teeth pulled a wisp of hay from the rack. There was hay in his forelock. He blinked sleepily.

'Come indoors and I'll clean your face up,' said Pippa.

'Nay. Swarms o' bluebottles gi' me the jumpies. A dab o' whiskey d'clane th' place, an' ol' cobbyweb d'stap the bleeden.'

'If you talk like that, I'll stop being sorry for you. Who exactly is this Libby person?'

'Miss Elizabeth Franklin, manager and chief instructor of a local riding school, engaged to be married to a dashing fellow, a lady of excellent repute.'

'Oh. How is she involved in all this?'

'She is only marginally involved, as my friend.'

'But…'

'She wishes you well.' Dan Mallett stood up. He seemed to be stiff, but in one piece. He looked battered and dishevelled and blood-spattered, and one of his brilliant blue eyes was completely hidden by a puffy purple lid.

'You can't just go!' said Pippa.

'Ay,' said Dan, drawing out the syllable as slow as syrup, reverting to this other voice to cheer Pippa up, she thought: perhaps to cheer himself up. 'Me mam been worreten.'

Suddenly he had disappeared. He was through the stable door and away. His feet made no sound on the flagstones of the yard. There was a little shuffle and a metallic clang, and a small insect clicking of a bicycle chain on its sprockets.

He had not kissed her. Pippa supposed this was because his face was covered in blood. She thought she would not have minded a bit of blood.

'Trouble with the horses, Miss Lees?'

'No,' said Pippa, startled.

'I thought I heard a bit o' banging about.'

'Just, um, a bit of banging about.'

'All serene now?'

'Yes, thank you.'

Pippa went upstairs, wondering why she had not told them anything about it.

She was tired of being disbelieved, and she was frightened of the man with the knife.

She looked at herself in the mirror, in the small pale characterless bedroom. She looked tousled but normal. She was often tousled after filling the stable buckets or getting hay from the loft. She did not look as though she had just been attacked and terrorized and threatened. It was extraordinary that such an experience should leave no visible sign. It was almost unfair.

Photographs, she thought, sleepless in the dark, her wrists and arms rather remembering pain than feeling it, her mind troubled and frightened in spite of there being so many policemen so near.

They were funny about photographs in this house, about the ones they had and the ones they did not have. In the downstairs cloakroom there were all the usual photographs of officers' messes and polo teams and country house parties arranged on lawns, and none was more recent than the mid-1930s.

There were none of Jack Marriner.

Very rum.

As she went at last to sleep, Pippa posted into her subconscious a card noting the oddity of there being no photographs of Jack Marriner, and beside it a card noting the curious, unexplained importance of that one photograph — print and negative both — missing from the packet of humdrum photographs of the previous autumn.

And in the morning, her subconscious had printed a photograph of Jack Marriner on to that blank card.

That was who the missing photograph was of.

Everything went clickety-click in Pippa's brain as she pulled on a dressing-gown and went downstairs to let the dogs out. Click.

They never did get that money back, after Jack Marriner disappeared. They never did find out what happened to all the money.

Click.

He never did drown himself, did he? It was like that MP who left his clothes on the beach, not like Robert Maxwell. He never had the least intention of drowning. He made arrangements to get himself over to France, with all that money in a canvas bag. He lost himself in a big town, and bought himself an identity in a shop where identities were sold, and lived safely and secretly ever after, until —

Click.

Last autumn, when by accident or design he ran into Mary Craik in Brittany, where she was on holiday with her horrible friends.

Click.

He might have grown a beard, but she recognized him. She knew he was alive, and living on a lot of stolen money.

Click.

What was it they said about him? He was the dancer, the exhibitionist, the show-off. His fancy footwork danced him out of trouble, until one day he had to jump his way out of it, over the side of his boat, but he surfaced and danced again. He was the shadow dancing on the ceiling, and he boasted about his cleverness on the telephone, and he danced on the gravel in the middle of the night, just to be clever, just to hug himself for his cleverness. It all fitted. It was the same recognizable, cocky, conceited, amoral, unreliable, consistent personality. A horrible man. A horrible smarmy voice on the telephone in the middle of the night, and from the dark in the back seat of the car. A man with a big sharp knife, a bully who gagged and threatened girls in stables...

Click.

Mary Craik photographed him in Brittany, having met him by accident or design. And then what? Lo and behold, she's driving a lovely new Volvo.

Click.

She was blackmailing him. She could do it with that photograph. It was all she needed. The threat of showing somebody that photograph, and saying when it was taken.

Click.

She was meeting him in this house, his wife's house, that night when his wife had gone away. He telephoned to make sure that Judith really was away. Mary Craik came in person to check that Judith really was away.

He telephoned and heard the yapping of the dachshund. He knew it was a dachshund. How could he know that? Because it had been his dog.

Jacob had been his dog, so he could catch it and take it away and bring it back and tie it to a gatepost. Very few people in the world could have done that, but he could.

He had keys to the house and to the annexe. He could let himself into the annexe and use the telephone, immediately after he had wired little Jacob to the gatepost. He got Mary Craik to that chair by the telephone. He knew all about that. It had been his chair and his telephone.

He knew where everything was in the house and the yard and the outbuildings, because it had been his house.

He made an appointment to meet Mary Craik at a time when Judith was away. They could not meet in her house, in case her husband came in.

Mary Craik was excited, seething and popping with excitement, looking forward avidly to meeting him.

Yes, not because he was her lover but because he was her meal-ticket. She was avid for money. She had probably never had very much, and what she had had Michael Craik had spent...

Mary Craik had not worried about Pippa seeing Jack Marriner. Pippa had no idea what Jack looked like. There was no photograph of him in the house. He had been careful, perhaps, to remove any trace of himself before he disappeared, in order that he could disappear. He would know that Judith was not likely to paper the walls with pictures of him.

Of course, Pippa never did see him, because of his manoeuvre with the dachshund.

Click.

Dan Mallett knew. Somehow, Dan Mallett had known all along. That was why the creature Libby's discovery about the bicycle did not interest him. It was irrelevant. Michael Craik had taken a long time to relieve himself, that was all. Possibly he had been drinking a lot of beer, or he had a chill on his bladder.

Dan Mallett knew, and he had been telling Pippa. He had nudged her towards understanding.

Why had he done that, instead of simply telling her?

Pippa thought she understood. She thought she was becoming used to the subtle, overcomplicated ways in which Dan Mallett's mind worked, such as his prediction to his mother that Pippa would appear at the cottage. In this case, she would never have believed it about Jack Marriner, if Dan had simply told her that he was alive and rich and a murderer. She believed this because she had arrived at the truth on her own. At least, she could kid herself that she had got there on her own.

Dan Mallett was a sophisticated operator. Pippa felt awed. She felt irritated that she should have been manipulated so smoothly.

From the back door, Pippa stood looking across the yard to the stable, waiting for the dogs to come in. Dan Mallett came out into the yard. His face was cleaned up, but it was a mess. His left eye was purple and completely closed, his lip was split, and there was a piece of sticking plaster on his right cheek and another on his forehead.

He limped as he came out of the stable. There was a bandage round his right hand and a plaster across the back of his left.

'Evils o' drink,' said the policeman on duty by the door, following Pippa's eye.

'What?'

'Frackarse arter closin' time, in the car-park o' the Chestnut Horse. The man 'isself told us. A breach o' the peace were committed, speakin' strictly by the letter o' the law, but no bones was broken, an' the alleged offence were committed on private property, so proceeding will not be taken. Pity, really.'

'Why a pity?'

''Cos 'e's the biggest villain unhung, that bloke,' said the policeman vaguely, as though repeating a mantra of discredited authority.

Dan Mallett had also lied to them about the battle in the stable. It was just as well for them both that they both had.

Pippa stared across the yard at the battered, disreputable little figure, apparently so frail, apparently so simple. She felt new, strong, complicated emotions.

Amidst these emotions, generally pleasant, a question spiked itself which was thoroughly unpleasant: Where was Jack

Marriner? Where was he living, under what identity? He must be some way off. He must be among people who had never seen him. Did he come here in a car, when he came? He came pretty often. Where did he leave his car? Whose car was it? Had anybody seen a strange car? Had he only ever come in the middle of the night, except when he was murdering people or terrorizing house-sitters? Would he come again? Where did he think the photograph was? Could he be trapped?

Dan Mallett saw Pippa looking at him. He waved. He did not grin. No doubt it was painful to grin, with that cut lip. Pippa did not know whether to wave back, to betray friendship in front of the policeman; but, before she could decide, she found that she had already waved.

The policeman also waved. He thought Dan's greeting had been for him. His wave was patronizing. He thought he was waving to the village idiot.

Pippa saw that Jack Marriner would come back. He would come for that one missing photograph. Jack Marriner was not safe until he had that photograph, until he destroyed it, print and negative both.

He had already murdered for that photograph. He would do so again. So the photograph was the bait that would catch him. Pippa had to convey that she had the photograph. Maybe he already thought she had it, perhaps only that she knew where it was.

The police would not believe a word of any of this. They did not believe a word she said, or a word Dan Mallett said.

There was no end to their trouble or their danger, until Jack Marriner walked into a trap.

Pippa had to make herself the bait.

CHAPTER 12

'Some of the people in the village are still saying Dan Mallett did it,' said the Libby person.

'He couldn't kill anybody!' said Pippa.

Libby laughed. 'Oh yes he could. He did. I was there when he killed someone. He killed two people.'

'How?' said Pippa, astonished by the girl's calmness.

'With a swarm of bees. He killed two gangsters with a lot of bees.'

'But not a woman. How could anybody think that? That he could kill a woman with a poker, and then a cushion over her face?'

'A poker...' The Libby person laughed. 'I knocked him out with a poker, once. That was how we met, really.'

'Why did you?'

'Why did I hit him with a poker? Because I thought he was a burglar.'

'Was he?'

'Yes, he was.' Libby laughed again. 'Of course he was.'

They were in the little newsagent's shop, almost buried under cigarettes and plastic buckets and cheap brown envelopes and chocolate bars, and the conversation of the woman with coconut-matting hair, and the misery of Mr Lewis, the proprietor.

The woman introduced the two girls to one another, making a large social event out of a chance meeting in the little shop.

'I ought to explain about that saddle,' said Libby Franklin. 'I would have asked you, but I didn't know you existed. I've been borrowing stuff for ... well, Judith Marriner doesn't know what's in the saddle room and what isn't. Dan has always looked after the tack. She leaves it to him. She never uses any of it. I don't think she's ever ridden.'

'I don't believe she ever has,' said the woman of the shop, impatient at being silent for so long. 'Never a foot in the stirrup or a you-know-what on the saddle, heigh ho, heigh ho, a-hunting we will go, not for her, though, or am I thinking of *Snow White and the Seven Dwarfs?*'

'Sleepy, one 'o them was,' said Mr Lewis tragically. 'I wish some others were a bit more like him, not a million miles from 'ere.'

'There it goes again,' said the woman. 'The flashin' rapier. The quickness of the hand deceives the eye. I don't know how he does it, truly I don't. I do remember the episode to which you 'ave reference, Miss Franklin, quite a local sensation that was, same like this little accident befell our Mrs Craik.'

'Not a thing to joke about,' said Mr Lewis.

'Have you seen Dan Mallett today?' Pippa asked Libby Franklin.

'No.'

'It might be a shock.'

'Nothing about Dan Mallett shocks anybody who knows him.'

'He, hm, hit his face on something last night.'

'Somebody's husban', I dessay,' said Mr Lewis. 'Dunno why it don't happen more often.'

'Did he really kill two people?'

'Oh yes,' said the woman, before Libby had a chance to reply. 'I remember like it was yesterday. There was some said he did the right thing. But o' course, wi' Dan Mallett, there's always some say he never did the right thing in 'is life.'

In the road outside the shop, Libby Franklin said, 'I'm not sure where my duty lies.'

'Your duty?' said Pippa.

'I'm torn between my duty to the female sex and my duty to Dan Mallett.'

'Have you got a duty to Dan Mallett?'

'Of course I have.'

'You said he was being a burglar when you met him?'

'Yes.'

'Is he often?'

'It doesn't matter. It's not the important thing about him, whether he's a burglar or not.'

'Oh,' said Pippa. 'What is the important thing about him?'

'Surely you know by now.'

'Hm. He's two people.'

'More.'

'His mother talks like he sometimes talks.'

'I think she puts it on a bit too,' said Libby Franklin. 'She's got a sense of humour.'

'But his other voice...'

'Oh, from the bank. Don't you know about his career?'

'Career? Dan? A *career*?'

'Oh, you don't know about him. It's high time you heard. Heavens, you must have been mystified. Dan's father was a poacher, right? Living in that cottage you've seen.'

Pippa nodded. So far she was not at all surprised.

'Then Dan got scholarships and things, and went to the grammar school, and got into the bank in Milchester, and spoke all BBC and wore a dark suit and a collar and tie, and took girls to the cinema, and there he was, headed for a directorship and everything...'

'How awful.'

'Yes, that's what he thought. He suddenly decided he wanted to live like his father. He dived back into the undergrowth. So half the time you're talking to a bank manager, and half the time you're talking to a stone-age poacher. It's confusing.'

'Yes,' said Pippa. She suddenly laughed. 'But it's interesting. Why does he come and do my job? Day after day, morning and evening, mucking out and everything, when I'm being paid to do it?'

'Oh, that,' said Libby. 'That you do understand.'

'No.'

'Don't pretend you don't understand *that*.'

'I promise I don't.'

'He saw you when you came here the first time, to see the place, to be interviewed by Judith Marriner.'

'He saw me? He wasn't there.'

'Of course he saw you. He sees everything. He's always there, here, there and everywhere. If a pretty girl pops up, anywhere for twenty miles round, Dan's there to have a look.'

'Oh.'

'That's why he comes and does the horses.'

'Well I'm damned,' said Pippa.

'Are you cross?'

'Yes. No.'

Libby laughed.

Pippa thought it her duty to tell the police about Jack Marriner. She thought also that, if the police watched out for him and caught him, then he would not kill her.

The Superintendent heard Pippa out, looking throughout not at her but at a corner of the ceiling. He said, 'I think I am right in supposing that you never met Mr Marriner, Miss Lees.'

'No. I mean, you are right.'

'Never spoke to him? Never heard his voice?'

'Er, no.'

'Has his voice been described to you? As high or low, fast, slow, with this or that tone or accent?'

'Um, well, no.'

'Yet you identify as his a voice you heard on the telephone.'

'It might sound a bit far-fetched, but...'

'The intruder whose footstep you say you heard. It was dark. It was in the small hours of the morning. You were in bed. You did not see the person. You did not see whether male or female, tall or short, white or Black. You yourself have said that you heard only the crunch of a foot on gravel.'

'Yes, well, but...'

'And you can by some magic technique, denied to the rest of us, identify the footsteps as Mr Marriner's.'

'Well, there's a bit more to it...'

'The missing photograph. You have not seen it. You have not heard it described, because nobody has seen it. But you know what it depicts.'

'Yes, well, it's only logical, think of that Volvo...'

'Thank you for your assistance, Miss Lees. It is very public-spirited of you to help the police in their investigations. May I ask you, however, to wait until we consult you, before you favour us with your discoveries?'

After this snub, Pippa might not have bothered to catch the murderer, to do the job of the wretched police for them. But until she caught him, she was in danger. The killer thought she knew more than she did, that she even had the photograph. She was only safe when she was actually in the company of a policeman. Life could not be lived on those terms.

'Ah, Miss Lees,' said a gentle, insinuating voice from the middle of a bush.

Pippa started violently, causing Jacob to bark and Mr Tomkins to charge at her shins with messages of comfort and love.

'I thought you might come this way, because Jacob likes coming this way.'

Pippa looked carefully all around. She was alone with the dogs and with Dan Mallett.

Dan was now just visible, in the thin January sunshine, in the ragged shrubbery below the garden. He was slightly more of a mess than in the morning, because he had been roosting in the bush.

'I'm not here,' said Dan Mallett. 'I'm in Milchester, probably disposing of stolen goods. Nobody knows I'm here. Everybody knows I've gone to Milchester. It's Mr Tomkins you're talking to; he's got a burr in his tail, poor little fellow.'

'Why?'

'Why has he got a burr in his tail? It happens to King Charles spaniels more than to any other breed. I don't know why. Plumy tail, carried low, frequently waved to express adoration.'

'I mean, why are you hiding? Who from?'

'Ah. That's what I wanted to discuss. I understand you've done the sum, but the gentlemen in blue don't believe you.'

'How can you possibly know what I said to the Superintendent?'

'He and I are old and intimate friends.'

'I simply don't believe you.'

'No. He wouldn't put it the way I put it. Our paths have often crossed, to the extent that we communicate telepathically. He knows things about me I wish he didn't, and I know what goes on around him.'

'I suppose you seduced one of those women policemen.'

'Policepersons? How about that, to be a bit more logical? Woman policeman is ridiculous.'

'Oh, shut up,' said Pippa, whose feet were getting cold from standing still. 'Why are you hiding in a bush?'

'No other cover suggests itself.'

'I shall get cross in a minute. Why are you hiding?'

'Your friend of last night won't appear again if he thinks I am on the spot. I don't know why, he's bigger than both of us. But he's certainly more likely to come and see you if he thinks I'm in Milchester.'

'Come and see me,' said Pippa. She gulped. She spoke as though to Mr Tomkins. She squatted down, as though to pull burrs out of the feathers of his legs. She was not sure why she was, to this point, obeying Dan Mallett's instructions.

'Come and see you,' said Dan Mallett, 'in the hope of recovering the photograph which proves he's still alive.'

'Yes. I'm scared.'

'So would I be. You're thinking of making yourself into a bait to catch him, is that right?'

'How did you know that?'

'It's what I would have done, in your place, if I'd had the guts. You're a great girl. You're really brave.'

'Oh,' said Pippa, extraordinarily pleased.

'None of this can be proved unless we actually catch him and hold him up to the light in front of people who know who he is.'

'That's what I thought.'

'What made you realize?'

'I don't know. I slept on it. It all added up. It's all in character, all the frilly bits on the edges, all the show-off bits. The telephone and the footsteps, the clever-clever bits. The timing adds up. Brittany, then the car... The other people she was with, the people in the photograph...'

'Ugly mugs, weren't they?'

'Did they see Jack Marriner?'

'If they did, they didn't know it was him they were seeing. They were from distant places, from her ancestral pastures. Melton Mowbray or some such. Grim and grey I imagine, full of people with too many teeth.'

'Teeth,' repeated Pippa blankly.

'You know what I mean. People with mouths excessively full of teeth. It gives their speech an arrogant quality, much disliked by the peasantry.'

'My God, you do talk.'

'It's nervousness,' said Dan Mallett comfortably. 'The point is that, as far as I know, Mary Craik was the only person in the world who knew Jack Marriner was alive, and living abroad on the ample fruits of his crimes.'

'Did he know she knew?'

'As soon as she started to blackmail him, yes, of course he knew. That's why he killed her. I don't think he knows you know, and I don't think he knows I know. He thinks we think it's somebody else who killed Mary Craik, and threatened you with a knife, and gave me this mouse. I might think it was Michael Craik, same as the bluebottles do.'

'They don't think that, because...'

'You might think it was me, on account of being friends with little Jacob.'

'Well, I... The police couldn't possibly think Michael Craik did it.'

'They've thought so all along. He had an alibi, but it wasn't a very good one.'

'He's got no alibi at all. I told them. They couldn't have cared less. They weren't interested in that business about the bicycle.'

'They'd already guessed about a bicycle. It was obviously a way Michael Craik could have got here, quick and quiet. It didn't have to be Curly Godden's bike. Any old bike would do. Not mine, perhaps.'

'Then why was the Super so beastly when I told him?'

'Doesn't like amateur contributions. Reads too many mystery novels. Identifies with the bobby in Sherlock Holmes and the bobby in Poirot, you know, when the bluebottles are outsmarted by the amateurs. It's very humiliating for a policeman.'

'That's just silly.'

'Not altogether. They did guess about the bicycle.'

'Well, they won't have it that Jack Marriner's alive.'

'They will when we've caught him.'

'Am I supposed to trust you? After what Libby said?'

'In the ordinary way I'd advise you not to, but this time I think you'll have to.'

'Did you actually save my life last night?'

'Oh, don't let's exaggerate.'

'Hmm,' said Pippa. 'How did you come to realize Jack Marriner was alive?'

'I started from the point when Mary Craik was waiting at the rendezvous. When she was here, with you. All avid, you said she was.'

'Yes. I thought she was feeling sexy.'

'But who for? Who could that be? Mary Craik with a secret admirer? With all those enlarged pores in her nose? I just couldn't believe it.'

'Don't be foul. She's dead.'

'She had to be avid for something other than caresses,' said Dan, from the middle of the bush. 'And I thought it might be money. When I got to that point, my mind started working the same way yours did.'

'It was very clever of us both,' said Pippa.

Dan looked at her from his bower of tatty evergreen foliage, one large and startling blue eye and one grossly swollen shiner. He sketched a grin, which obviously hurt him.

'Why does Jack Marriner think I've got the photograph?' asked Pippa suddenly.

'Because you found the other ones. You found them in a drawer.'

'Yes. I still don't understand that. Why were the kitchen scissors there? There are still too many things I don't understand.'

'There are things about this business you'll never understand, not until the day you die.'

'I hope that's not today.'

'It's something we must try to prevent. For the moment you'd better proceed with your friends there, so that if he's watching he won't be suspicious. Bun doesn't want a walk, but the others do. You could have taken five thousand teazles out of five thousand dogs in the time you've been hanging about talking.'

'In the time *I've* been...'

'Besides, I expect you're getting cold.'

Pippa was dismissed, and sent off on her walk with the dogs.

Her feet were, in truth, so cold by now that she could hardly walk on them. She hobbled away across the rough grass with the dogs, Jacob leading the way, Mr Tomkins cavorting round her ankles, old Bunbury following with a resigned air of humouring the rest of them.

Pippa did not expect to be attacked by Jack Marriner in broad daylight. He would not risk showing himself in a place where he had lived, where he was well known. He would not risk going about the countryside under the pale glare of the sun. But as soon as it got dark…

He had already killed one woman to get that photograph.

'Hallo, Pippa Lees?'

Pippa recognized the high, clear voice of the Libby person. She knew that a policewoman was monitoring the call from the annexe.

Libby was Dan Mallett's intimate ally and confidante. She borrowed Judith Marriner's expensive tack on the strength of being Dan's friend, which was stretching things a bit, taking advantage, thoroughly dishonest. Dan had probably told Libby about Jack Marriner. She probably believed him, because she probably believed everything he told her. Perhaps he quite often told her the truth, although he was generally reckoned a man who would tell lies to a gatepost, simply to keep in practice.

'I'm ringing on behalf of Dan Mallett,' said Libby, 'because he hasn't got a telephone.'

'Um,' said Pippa, wondering whether to warn Libby that the police were listening in.

'I know the police are plugged into this call,' said Libby, before Pippa had decided what to say. 'But we don't need to worry about that, do we, as we're not doing anything wrong? Quite the reverse, we're doing a public service.'

This Libby was as gabby as Dan Mallett himself, thought Pippa crossly. Would she never get to the point?

'Dan says he's sorry, he can't come to do the horses this evening. But he'll be there in spirit.'

Pippa took this to mean that he would be there in hiding.

'Our missing friend will have an interesting face,' said Libby.

Pippa wondered what the listening policewoman would make of this gnomic remark. Pippa interpreted it as meaning that Jack Marriner would be showing signs of the fight, which would prove a lot of things.

'We'd arrange for some other friends to meet him,' said Libby, 'but he always seems to know if anything's been arranged.'

This was true. Jack Marriner had shown himself awfully well-informed. He knew where people were going to be, and when. He was always popping up in stables and the backs of cars. He had a hiding-place on the spot or a local informer or a sixth sense or something.

It was amazing that he remained so invisible when he was so constant a presence.

Pippa realized that, ever since she had arrived in this horrible place, she had had the sense of being watched.

She could no longer feel safe even with the dogs, even in broad daylight. The dogs knew and trusted Jack Marriner.

The fatal photograph with which Mary Craik had blackmailed Jack Marriner, for which he had killed her — he thought Pippa had it. If she had really had it, she would have shown it to the police, because it explained everything and let them all off a hook. Why did he think she had not done that?

Because he thought she was going to try to blackmail him too. That was the way his mind worked. She had not started to blackmail him yet because he was on the spot, invisible, unsuspected, and he would kill her. That was what he did to people who blackmailed him. But the time would come when she would be safe from him, and then she would turn the screws and be able to buy expensive new Volvo cars. That was the way Jack Marriner's mind was certainly working.

And someone else might get hold of that photograph, and have copies of it made, so there would be other blackmailers, no end to his troubles. He had to get hold of it.

Two murders carried no more penalty than one murder.

It was not obvious why he thought Pippa had the photograph.

Pippa was made to feel almost as though she did have it. She imagined the photograph as showing Jack Marriner sitting at a cafe table beside a road, under an umbrella advertising Cinzano, perhaps, or a red-and-white striped awning. He would be wearing an open-necked shirt, and drinking a pastis or a Kir.

He would think himself so camouflaged as to be invisible, blending entirely with his surroundings, except for somebody who knew he had been drowned in the Channel.

Pippa felt as though she could see the photograph, so vividly did she imagine it, extrapolating from all the other photographs in that packet, the ordinary holiday snapshots.

Pippa brought the horses in, in the last of the daylight. She was frightened, going into the looseboxes and the tack-room and the hayloft. She knew Dan Mallett was nearby, but she did not try to communicate with him. Jack Marriner was probably also nearby, and he would be alerted to Dan's hidden presence, and the plan would fail.

Pippa fed the horses and filled their hay-racks and water-buckets. She put the stable-rug on Cavendish. She did all this with her chin on her shoulder, in a mood of suffocating suspense, aware of being watched, aware of imminent danger.

Nothing happened.

When she had finished, she still waited for the attack, needlessly hanging about in the stable, inventing fiddly jobs to give an excuse for lingering, waiting for the murderer to walk into their trap.

Nothing happened.

A sense of anti-climax descended like a fog.

Would he be here when she tucked up the horses for the night? Would Dan Mallett be here? Would she dare to come out to the stable at midnight?

Pippa went out again at eleven thirty. She was vividly alert, edgy, listening and looking. She tried to hide all this, out of pride, and in case Jack Marriner was watching her, in case he suspected the trap. She did not think she was hiding her nervousness very well.

She felt, telepathically, the hidden presence of Dan Mallett. She hoped it was his presence she felt, not merely the hope of it. The sense of his being there was deeply comforting. It was the only comfort in a situation otherwise revolting.

Nothing happened.

Pippa went to bed glad that there were policemen in the house. Nothing happened during the night.

Nothing happened in the morning, when Dan Mallett again neglected the horses in favour of hiding in ambush.

'This can't go on,' said Dan Mallett. 'It's too tiring for you, all that hard labour in the stable.'

'I don't mind doing the horses,' said Pippa. 'But I get cold shivers up my spine.'

'Yes, of course you do, but you don't show it, and that makes you the bravest girl I ever knew.'

'Oh…'

'The bravest and the nicest and the most desirable.' Dan smiled, although it still evidently hurt him to smile. In spite of his swollen black eye and his cuts and bruises and sticking-plasters, his smile was gently lecherous, caressing and arousing and sweet. 'I think we'd better let the great big boobies in blue into our secret,' he said. 'Then they can make themselves responsible for looking after you.'

'I have let them into our secret,' said Pippa. 'They didn't believe a word of it. For instance, they said, how could I have recognized Jack Marriner's voice on the telephone when I'd never met him? They missed the point completely.'

'Yes, that could have been predicted. But now there's something we know that they don't yet know.'

'What?'

'He tried to scrag you in the stable, and gave me this cosmetic surgery. And he said at the time, by way of explaining, that what he wanted was the photograph.'

'I wondered whether to tell them about that.'

'Why didn't you?'

'I was scared he'd find out I'd told them. He would, too. I'm still scared of telling them, because he'll find out, because he finds out everything, and next time you might not be there…'

Dan took Pippa's hand. She returned the grip of his fingers. She continued to be surprised, even shocked, at what was happening to her, but it was sure enough happening. She had a great and unmaidenly desire to kiss his small, battered face, but she did not know if there was any part of his face which she could kiss without hurting him.

'They'll put a guard on you,' said Dan. 'I will too, as much as I can.'

'I feel safer with you,' said Pippa.

'Do you? I must be getting old.'

'I feel horribly unsafe with you,' Pippa hastened to reassure him, 'but that's not what I'm talking about.'

'We must get them looking in the right direction,' said Dan. 'While things go on as they are, none of us has time for anything important. I think we'd better form up to my friend Brer Fox.'

The Detective Chief Superintendent did look more than usually like a fox as he stared over a desk-top at Dan and Pippa.

Dan cringed. He became smaller and humbler and more like a scruffy little mongrel dog: more like a peasant somehow left behind, in the rural rockpool, by the tide of history.

Pippa understood that his performance was valuable to him in his dealings with authority.

'About this photograph,' said the Super.

'A b'lieves a-did yere a-ben talk o' photy,' said Dan very slowly and sweetly, with an air of baffled innocence.

Pippa restrained herself from giggling, but it was a near thing.

'Oh, come on, Mallett,' said the Super. 'You know exactly what I'm talking about.'

'A yeard talken,' Dan admitted.

'You have seen the photograph?'

'Nay.'

'But you conclude that it depicts the late Mr Marriner.'

'A d'believe it do.'

'Who is therefore not the late Mr Marriner at all, but an embezzler on the run, presumably living in France.'

'I did tell you that,' said Pippa.

'There seems to be some merit in your account, Miss Lees.'

'Yes, I know there is. The merit of our account is that it's true. What made you change your mind?'

'I have not changed my mind. It has been, and remains, open to various possibilities. Mallett here is a grossly unreliable source of information...'

'Ay,' said Dan, as though delighted by a rare compliment.

'But on this occasion his story has to be taken seriously, in view of the fight, which you now report, in the stable. You should have told us about that immediately, Miss Lees.'

'I was scared to.'

'You were scared of Marriner's displeasure. I understand that. We know what he does to people who displease him. But now you have told us because you are scared not to. That is wise.'

'Ay,' said Dan. 'A did say t' th' maidie 'at a-bent able fur t' stand senterry go twantyfur owerrs o' day.'

What Dan said was true and reasonable, Pippa thought, but she thought the way he said it was grossly over the top. Surely a clever, fox-like policeman would see that he was putting it on?

But the Super said seriously, 'Miss Lees will be safe if she is sensible and obedient.'

Dan winked at Pippa. She had great difficulty in keeping a straight face. It was silly, because the danger she was in was extremely real.

'We want that photograph, Miss Lees.'

'So does Jack Marriner.'

'I wish I could be sure that you do not have it.'

'It must be somewhere about. Mary Craik must have had it.'

'And Marriner knew she had it. She sent him an extra print, perhaps. He paid her a certain sum, with which she brought a nice new car. Then she made a further demand, and he realized there would be no end to it. He reacted as I myself would perhaps have done, if I had found myself the victim of blackmail. But he embellished his reaction, if I may so put it, by a characteristic display of gratuitous cleverness, a kind of ostentatious elegance which should have been risk-free while it caused him the greatest gratification. Rather a silly man. Rather a nasty one.'

'It does all fit, doesn't it?' said Pippa, trying not to sound smug.

'It bears a kind of signature, yes.'

'You do believe all that, then? Everything I told you?'

'It has been established as one among several possibilities, Miss Lees,' said the Detective Chief Superintendent coldly, not yet willing to admit that he had been wrong.

'Gum,' said Dan Mallett, in a tone of wondering admiration, ''at's gurt big wordies.'

Pippa had to give a large imitation sneeze into her handkerchief in order to hide her laughter.

'Now Michael Craik's disappeared,' said an evergreen shrub at the bottom of the orchard.

'Eek,' said Pippa, startled into biting her tongue, and causing Jacob to bark like a lunatic. 'Are you still hoping to trap him?'

'I'm watching over your goings and comings,' said the bush. 'I can't do it all the time, but I can still do it some of the time.'

'Oh, thank you.'

'I like watching you, as you know. I would like to watch more of you, more of the time. That's for later. Meanwhile, as I say, Michael Craik has disappeared. I think it means he's found the photograph. He's trying to use it the way his wife did. But he doesn't want to end up the way she ended up. So he's somehow got a message to Jack Marriner and put himself out of danger.'

'He's found the photograph, and he hasn't told the police?'

'Obviously not, if he's using it for blackmail.'

'How does he know how to get hold of Jack Marriner?'

'He must have found that too, with the photograph. A telephone number, an accommodation address, something. Next thing you know, he'll be driving a Jaguar, if he's still alive, which he will be, since he's gone into hiding. Nobody's seen him for two or three days. It's only just dawned on the neighbours that he hasn't been visible. They often don't see him for days anyway. He's not a sociable fellow at the cottage-garden level, not one for exchanging pleasantries over the fence.'

'Then p'raps he hasn't disappeared, he's just stayed indoors.'

'No, he's sure enough gone away. The bluebottles are really keen to see the photograph, having accepted that it exists. Mary Craik might have put it in a safe-deposit or similar, but I think that kind of female would be more likely to squirrel it away under the undies in the back of a drawer in her bedroom.'

'Mm. I think that's probably right.'

'So do our bullet-headed friends in blue. So they're taking the wretched house apart brick by brick. Consequently, they observe the absence of the householder.'

'Well, I'm glad they don't think I've got it.'

'They may think there's more than one copy of the print,' said the bush. 'Jack Marriner may think so. They may all be right. Mary Craik might have had dozens of prints made, each one worth ten thousand quid of Jack Marriner's money.'

'Oh. Oh yes. Then I'm still the bait in the trap.'

'Sort of. That's why I'm here.'

'Do the police think so too? Am I the bait in their trap?'

'Yes, love. There's a conscientious officer watching you at this moment with a pair of binoculars, from an upstairs window of the house. He hopes you're in danger.'

'He's right.'

'Yes, he's right.'

Pippa shivered. Mr Tomkins the little spaniel whined, sensing her mood.

CHAPTER 13

'You will not go out without telling us, Miss Lees.'

'No, I won't,' said Pippa.

'You will be accompanied at all times, when you do go anywhere, by a police officer.'

'Yes. Literally everywhere? All the time? Even when I...?'

'You may not always be aware of the officer's presence. Even if you are aware of it, you will sometimes, if we ask you, ignore it.'

'Oh. I see. Trap. Yes. I hope whoever's there will be fairly near.'

'Your escort will be close enough, Miss Lees.'

'My minder.'

'Don't try to give him the slip, even to meet Dan Mallett.'

'Why should I want...' began Pippa crossly, but she felt herself blushing. 'I need paraffin for the Aladdin. I must go to the garage.'

'Sergeant Horne of the CID will be pleased to have a lift to the garage and back, if that is quite convenient.'

'Oh yes. How long is this going to go on?'

'Until we are sure you are out of danger.'

'Jack Marriner will want to go back to France.'

'Not without the photograph.'

'He's in danger himself. He must be, as long as he's here, wherever he is. He must be very close. Any moment somebody might see him, somebody local who knows him.'

'Yes. It is true that he is showing great ingenuity. It is hard to see how he is managing it, keeping so close an eye on affairs here without ever showing his face. He is living up to his presentation of himself, his persona, as a sort of elusive Harlequin. He is very, very good at it. That is not a thought which, in your place, I would find reassuring.'

'You are a comfort,' said Pippa crossly.

The Detective Chief Superintendent smiled a cold, foxy smile. He wanted Pippa to be the obedient cheese in his trap.

'Miss Lees, as I live an' breathe,' said the man at the garage, who still appeared to have been stripped of a layer of skin, and who was scantily dressed for the weather. 'Long time no see. A squirt of parry-warry in the plastic container? No sooner said than done. I see you proceeds under guard. Riding shotgun, is he? What a shock all this will be for Mrs Marriner, when she gets back 'ere amongst us all, findin' the ancestral mansion crawlin' wi' minions o' the law, if minions is the word I 'as in mind, such mind as there is to 'ave it in. Myrmidons, would I be intendin'? A very fancy word, that, I wish I knew ezackly what it meant. There's five litres gone glug-glug into the vessel. Another five? No sooner saided than doneded. I didn't 'ave a chance to vouchsafe to Mrs M. any whisper o' melodramatic 'appenin's in 'er boudoir, so to say, when she honoured us wi' a tinkle two days ago.'

'Mrs Marriner telephoned? You talked to her?'

'Jangle-jangle, hallo hallo? A gabble of Italian, or so I surmised, a strain o' distant music o' Latin character, puttin' the listener in mind o' gondoliers an' such... Meet me at the airport, she says, peremptory like normal, mentionin' a date and time which I recorded on a bit o' pinky paper. Ho! I think I bin a trifle remiss.'

'You were supposed to tell me,' said Pippa.

'Well, I daresay I might have remembered, nearer the time. I'm ever so sorry. It's still five days away, nex' Tuesday the ninth, twelve noon approx, the great bird will descend from the sky wi' a roar o' jets an' the fanfare o' brass bands, an' the snortin' chariot will await 'er 'ighness, driven by my colleague Denis the Menace, who loves to act as retainer to the great and good.'

'Noon next Tuesday the ninth,' said Pippa. 'She'll be here by mid-afternoon.'

''Avin' been apprised o' the local scandals, by Denis the Menace, on root. A strange 'omecomin', eh? Findin' your domestic 'earth the scene o' gory murders. Ten litres finest quality parry, pink in colour to distinguish it from rival brands. Yes, I'll take the Visa same like always as per usual. Tata then, lovely to 'ave another chinwag.'

'That bloke,' said the Detective Sergeant as Pippa drove away, 'says every single ruddy thing anybody ever 'eard of, 'ceptin' the one thing he was supposed to say, which was tellin' you when Mrs Marriner was comin' back.'

'Never mind. We know now.'

'Very rum, her givin' the garage a bell, an' not botherin' to tell you.'

'She gave them a message to tell me.'

'Yes, miss, but as a point o' courtesy…'

'No harm done.'

'Would that be in character, if I may venture to ask the question?'

'I hardly know Mrs Marriner.'

The Detective Sergeant nodded. He understood that Pippa was telling him that Judith Marriner's arrogant off-handedness was exactly in character.

'In five days' time,' said Dan Mallett. 'Oh. Your employment will be at an end. You'll fold your tent.'

'Yes.'

'And go to somewhere awful, like London.'

'I suppose so.'

'Awful in being distant. Five days. That's what we've got.'

'Oh my God,' said Pippa, suddenly aghast, suddenly realizing what was happening. 'That's what we've got. Is your face terribly sore?'

'Curate's egg. Some parts better than others.'

'I, um, need your help,' said Pippa. 'Fixing, um, a shelf upstairs.'

'I'll get some camouflage,' said Dan. He disappeared into the tool-shed, and came out with a saw and a hammer and a piece of plank.

Pippa tried to say something, but she was too excited to speak. She had never behaved in so shamelessly practical, so matter-of-fact a way before, in the run-up to what they were running up to. Usually there were low lights and expensive dinners and so forth. Now there was the broad merciless light of mid-afternoon, agreement reached in a couple of sentences, and the trappings of a couple of tools and a plank. It all seemed quite right. It was sensible and time-saving, and almost unbearably exciting.

Why hem and haw and muck about and waste time? There was little enough time. Minutes were precious. Quick, quick!

There was no shadow of doubt in Pippa's mind about what she wanted. There was none in Dan's. He smiled painfully, and sweetly and lecherously, as they started across the yard to the house.

'It's a shelf in the fitted cupboard in the spare room,' said Pippa with unnecessary loudness, her voice ringing terribly false in her own ears as they passed the policeman stationed at the back door.

'Shalf to fitty cubbid,' repeated Dan, speaking in a sort of humble croon. 'Ay, missie, us'll fix un.'

The policeman glanced at Pippa, his face perfectly wooden. It was impossible to guess if he guessed. Pippa was sure he knew exactly what was going on. She felt her face flooded with a furious blush. She pretended to blow her nose, and walked very quickly and self-consciously upstairs.

'Bless Judith Marriner, in a manner of speaking,' said Dan, his head pillowed on Pippa's breast, his hair tickling her chin, his breath caressing the skin of her breast.

'Why, darling?' said Pippa dreamily, not ready at all to return from the Paradise to which Dan had so gently carried her.

'Bounced us into this bed,' murmured Dan. 'Accelerated matters wonderfully. How long would we have hung bashfully about, without that deadline?'

'Another six hours, I should think,' said Pippa.

Dan's torso, white and delicate-skinned, though remarkably muscled, was pressed against her hip, and his legs twined with her legs. One of his hands was on her thigh, one under her head. She felt his ribs softly vibrate with laughter.

'About another six minutes,' said Pippa.

Pippa put the kettle on in the kitchen. The dogs said it was their dinner time, but they lied.

Pippa thought it was a shame to get dressed. But it was too cold not to, and there were a number of things to do, such as the horses, and what was probably already obvious to the police would become blatant. She pulled her shapeless winter clothes on with reluctance, and with regret saw Dan's amazingly elegant body disappear into the ridiculous cocoon of his disguise.

She had five days for seeing it again. That was a really nice thought.

Dan and Pippa smiled at one another in the warm light of the kitchen, in the tolerant company of the dogs.

Pippa's broken heart was suddenly, miraculously healed. Dan was better than Fenton Lowell in every single way — more interesting, fuller of surprises, better looking, a better lover, better mannered, a more graceful mover, more stimulating, more restful, funnier, more honest in spite of being generally regarded as a rascal, more of a rascal...

While the kettle began to murmur that it was shortly going to boil, Pippa took down the orange-coloured kitchen scissors from their peg on the wall, in order to open a packet of ginger biscuits.

'That's where those things live?' said Dan, pointing at the hook.

'Yes.'

'And you always, without fail, put them back there?'

'Yes, so I know where to find them. It saves trouble.'

'But they got into one of these drawers?'

'This one.'

Dan opened it, revealing a jumbled miscellany of cast-off objects. He said, '*Could* you have put the scissors in here?'

'No. But I must have. Nobody else was in here after I'd last used them. None of the police came in here, in that time. I can't have put them in the drawer, but I must have.'

'You not only put them in the drawer, you hid them in the drawer.'

'Yes. I can't have. I must have.'

'You hid them under the photographs, the first batch.'

'Yes.'

The kettle boiled. Pippa made tea in a pot. Without thinking, she used Lapsang Souchong, not the black Indian tea from another jar on the dresser, the proletarian tea which Judith Marriner undoubtedly kept for gardeners, grooms and daily women.

Pippa simply assumed that anyone who made love as Dan did would want weak China tea with a slice of lemon.

'You guessed quite right,' said Dan.

They continued to smile foolishly at one another, although Dan was for some reason preoccupied by the kitchen scissors.

'Anybody who uses these things,' he said, 'uses them constantly. I suppose because so many things nowadays come wrapped in plastic. Maybe there are people who hack at the packaging with knives or choppers, but if you once get into the way of using these scissors, you use them several times a day.'

'Most days,' agreed Pippa. 'You certainly use them several times a week.'

'If they were missing, you'd search.'

'As I did.'

'As anybody would. That could be predicted. It was predicted. Why? What was the point? Why get you fossicking in drawers?'

'Well, why?'

'So that you'd find the photographs. Oh my, oh my, how stupid I think we've been. I do believe I begin to see.'

'What, darling?'

'And I begin to smell. Wow, ugh, what an overpowering pong.'

'My precious Dan, whatever are you gabbling about?'

'Surely you can smell it?'

'The tea?'

'The fish.'

'What fish?'

'The herring,' said Dan. 'The most gigantic and brilliant red herring.'

'I don't understand.'

'Nor do I. I must go away and think.'

'Can't you stay here and think?'

'No, love. I can't think with you in the room. You're hopelessly distracting. All I can think about is you. Some parts, I suppose, even more than others.'

'I shall never be able to think again,' said Pippa.

Dan grinned, kissed her, and slipped away into the gathering darkness.

Pippa subsided onto a kitchen chair, hugging to herself happy and shameless memories, and even more shameless predictions.

'I will not accompany you obtrusive, miss,' said the policeman on duty at the back door. 'Merely keep you under observation. I shall remain at all times within earshot, if so be as you has cause to cry out or exclaim.'

'Thank you,' said Pippa.

She had not expected to be so very glad to have a policeman as a nursemaid. But Dan was thinking. Pippa supposed he would not do his thinking in Judith Marriner's stable.

It was comforting that the police now thoroughly understood about Jack Marriner, and about his knife and about his photograph. Since she was the cheese in the trap, it was comforting that it was a big, powerful, well-manned trap, under the watchful eye of a lot of policemen.

Presumably Dan had gone home to do his thinking. Pippa hoped he would be quick about it. Time without him was time wasted, and they only had five days.

The air was colder. The sky in the west was green with the last of a cold sun.

The horses were in the far paddock. Pippa had opened the gate between the paddocks in the middle of the morning, so that the animals could go where they wanted. There was no reason to keep them in one field rather than another when they were only out for a few hours, and when there was no grass to speak of. She expected them to trot towards her as soon as they were aware of her. They came towards her, but only as far as the dividing gate. There they stopped. Somebody had shut the gate.

Who, and why?

The only people likely to bother with the gate, even to give it a moment's thought, were Dan and herself. She had not shut it, having taken the trouble to open it. She could not imagine why Dan would have done so without telling her. Anybody else could have shut the gate, approaching from the wood on the far side, and taking a bit of trouble to use the hedgerows as cover, without being seen from the house — using the horses as stalking-horses, perhaps: but what on earth would be the point?

Between the two paddocks was a post-and-rail fence, very smart, shaming the rest of the spread. The gate was in the corner, a normal field gate made of tubular metal sections, with a latch which could be opened one-handed but was proof against the pressure of a horse's nose. On the far side of the two paddocks ran a hedge of a kind typical of the area, a big mixed bullfinch, thorny but scraggy, punctuated by considerable trees. Once it had been kept clipped, perhaps cut-and-laid, but that was a long time ago. It was the sort of hedge nobody could jump over on a horse, but anybody could crawl through on hands and knees. The further gatepost was almost in the hedge. That was the end of the gate with the latch, so that the gate opened outwards, away from the hedge.

The winter darkness was falling quickly. It was high time to get the horses in.

Pippa felt a cold little whisper of alarm at the base of her spine. There was no reason for it. Dan had said she was brave. She tried to feel brave. The big solid policeman was by the back door, watching her, listening. The gate and the horses were hardly three hundred yards away. A scream would carry.

Jack Marriner could be hidden in the hedge by the gate. He could have got there unseen, and stayed there. But he couldn't stop Pippa screaming, and then the policeman would come running, and Jack Marriner would be seen and recognized and arrested, and that would be the end of everything for him.

Obviously, under these circumstance, Jack Marriner would not try anything, even if he was roosting in the hedge with his large knife. He would absolutely not dare.

Even so, Pippa wanted Dan.

Under the eye of the policeman, Pippa crossed the yard towards the gate of the nearer paddock. She unlatched and opened the first gate, leaving it wide for the horses. She started across the grass to the further gate. The horses watched her. Cavendish the big chestnut gelding was standing with his head over the gate, perhaps resting his neck on the top bar. Dorothy the old bay mare stood alertly, with her ears pricked, sending reproachful messages to Pippa that it was past her supper time. Talisman the nappy little dun stood a little apart from the others, as he always did, either because he thought himself inferior, or because he thought himself superior. He was alert too, but only half his attention was on Pippa.

Pippa glanced back at the house. They had switched on some lights indoors, so that the windows glowed rosily through the dusk. It looked welcoming and tranquil and traditional, a house on a Christmas card. Light blinked off the roofs of a couple of police cars parked beside the house.

Pippa strode towards the gate, her boots noiseless on the turf of the paddock. Cavendish raised his head from the gate and whickered softly. Dorothy flapped her ears. Talisman circled behind the other two.

Pippa reached the gate. She took off her glove to stroke Cavendish's nose, and to give him and Dorothy lumps of sugar. She pulled at the long, spring-loaded lever of the latch to open the gate for them. It was stuck. Something was holding the upright lever against the gatepost. It was not unheard of, that latches of this pattern jammed. It conveyed no special warning to Pippa. But she could not see what was wrong, or do anything about it, from where she was.

She climbed the gate. When she had a leg each side of the top bar, she heard a curious, powerful *whoomp* from the direction of the house, a sound like a giant pillow being hit by a heavy object. She twisted her head to look. She gave a yelp of amazement. A yellow-white flame was blooming skywards, like a crocus, from one of the police cars.

The car was not very near the house or the outbuildings, but it was near the other police car.

The dogs were indoors.

Pippa spent a split second thanking God that, at the moment of the explosion, she had not been leading the horses beside the car into the stable.

She spent another half-second wondering whether to stay with the horses, or run back to help, or what. She decided immediately that she ought to go back. She began to lift her right leg back over the top bar of the gate, when she felt it grabbed. There was a figure between the horses, a big man between the shoulders of Cavendish and Dorothy. He was holding her leg and now her waist. He pulled her off the gate into the far paddock where he was, where the horses were.

Pippa screamed.

'If you do that again, I'll kill you,' said Michael Craik. 'Even though they won't hear you because of our diversion.'

Even in this moment of crisis and terror, Pippa's brain seemed to be working. She realized that somebody, Michael Craik's accomplice, had set the car on fire. The effect was that the policeman by the back door would have run to the fire, or run indoors for help. He would certainly not have been watching her at the moment when she was grabbed. The noise and hubbub and excitement of that moment when the fire started would have drowned her one scream. Now if she screamed Michael Craik would kill her. He said so and she believed him.

She felt herself being dragged between the horses' legs beyond the gatepost to the fringe of the hedge. The two of them were now invisible from the house, as Michael Craik had been, even if the horses moved away.

He had a knife, a big kitchen knife with a broad blade and a sharp point. The light from the burning car gleamed on the bright blade of the knife. In the firelight, Pippa saw that Michael Craik's face was severely damaged. It was cut and bruised like Dan's, worse than Dan's.

Of course, it was Michael Craik who had attacked Pippa in the stable.

Why?

'Why?' said Pippa, very frightened, and hurt by the twisting of her arms behind her back.

'Now lie down,' said Michael Craik softly, smoothly, in the voice he had used on the telephone, the voice he had used in the back of Pippa's own car. 'Do exactly what you're told, or I'll kill you.'

Pippa sobbed and obeyed. She lay on her back in the bumpy and prickly fringe of the hedgerow, her head in a drift of dead leaves.

'In this story,' said Michael Craik, 'we kill people with cushions.'

'Some on us d'use shotty-guns,' said a gentle, treacly voice from the shadows, from a few yards up the hedge.

Dan. Dan had a gun. Thankfulness flooded Pippa like a tropical dawn.

Michael Craik moved with extraordinary speed. He loomed over Pippa, his knife in his hand. He put the point of the knife on her neck, below her chin, on the soft cotton collar of her polo-necked sweater.

'Now if anybody shoots me,' he said affably, 'I shall slump down on top of you, and my whole weight will be on the knife. I expect you remember the point. It's awfully sharp. You'd better tell your friend to be careful.'

'If you so much as scratch her, I'll blow your head off,' said Dan, in his other and educated voice.

The horses had wandered a few yards away, indifferent to incipient human death. Talisman was grazing, Cavendish looking apathetically at the lights of the house and the diminishing flames of the fire, Dorothy apparently asleep on her feet.

'Stalemate,' said Dan.

Pippa sobbed once, softly. She was angry with herself for showing this weakness.

'I suppose your idea was to do what Jack Marriner would have done, if he'd been here to do anything,' said Dan. 'Were you really going to kill the poor child?'

'As Jack Marriner would have done,' said Michael Craik equably, 'having recovered the photograph. He would have torn the picture of himself out of the photograph, and left the rest with the body, to show exactly what he'd done, to show how clever he'd been.'

'Torn the picture of himself out,' said Dan. 'The picture that never existed.'

Pippa squeaked with astonishment and disbelief. She squeaked softly. She was extremely conscious of the knife-point on her neck.

'My God, you were slow doing your sums about that photograph,' said Michael Craik. 'I thought you were never going to realize that Jack Marriner was alive and being blackmailed by my wife.'

'You would have given us a few more hints,' said Dan. 'You would have nudged us along.'

'We gave you plenty of hints as it was.'

'Telephone calls in the middle of the night,' said Dan, 'footsteps in the small hours, condescending giggles, all supposed to be consistent with Jack Marriner's perceived character.'

'It kept me up awfully late,' said Michael Craik. 'I lost a lot of sleep.'

'Then the photographs in the kitchen drawer,' said Dan, 'where Pippa was bound to find them. Then the second batch of photographs, turning up in your house. Big excitement, more photographs! It must mean something. What does it mean? And then you're saying that one photograph was missing. It was only you who said that. One missing, eh? Whatever can it be of? I wonder how on earth we ever came to swallow that,' said Dan. 'A man notices that one boring photograph is missing out of forty-eight boring photographs, taken five months before — how could anybody have believed that? But where you were clever was in making us think we were so wonderfully clever. That was what really convinced us, patting ourselves on the back. We tried to convince the police, but it was all too clever for them. So you nudged us a bit more, gave us a bit more evidence. You grabbed Pippa in the stable and started talking about photographs…'

'We wanted the police to believe in that photograph, that motive for the murder.'

'To believe Jack Marriner was alive and being blackmailed. Yes. You wanted the hapless bluebottles to devote all their energies, for the next fifty years, to scouring France for Jack Marriner, while you and Judith lived here in tranquillity and listened to the canaries.'

'She doesn't listen to the canaries much,' said Michael Craik. 'I'm more the one for that.'

'After our meeting in the stable, your face was much like mine,' said Dan. 'Which is why you went away, black eyes being apt to give rise to questions.'

'I wanted the cops to have the run of the house, anyway. To search it and not find anything.'

'"At were gurt brainsome,' said Dan, reverting for some reason to low comedy.

It was utterly extraordinary that these two men should be chatting, softly and reasonably, when one was pointing a gun at the other, and the other was pointing a knife at herself, and each would kill the other without hesitation or regret.

'Let me see if I fully understand,' said Dan, as though studying the instructions on a new electrical appliance. 'Your wife must have had much more money than anybody realized.'

'As of last October. An aunt's insurance policy matured. With copious bonuses, it came to a quarter of a million. So the woman bought herself a new car.'

'That was money you couldn't do without,' said Dan. 'You could cross the valley any time you liked, but not empty-handed. Your wife wasn't about to subsidize your bolting...'

'But, in the event, that is exactly what she has done,' said Michael Craik.

'Very adroit,' said Dan. 'Quite masterly. If your wife wasn't excited, that night, about getting money out of Jack Marriner, what was she excited about?'

'Meeting her boyfriend,' said Michael Craik. 'At least, that's what she thought she was going to do. That was the message she got. She was on the boil, wasn't she? Very enviable, really, to die in a condition of happy anticipation.'

'Who was it?' asked Dan.

'A waiter from one of the hotels they went to in Brittany. Aged nineteen, I believe. For sale to any bidder. She'd already given him several thousand quid. She was told he was coming to England, coming here. Judith was away. It all worked out lovely, a very romantic rendezvous. Scrubby little story, isn't it, a toy-boy from a hotel kitchen? Tell me, why did you expect this evening's escapade?'

'I thought you'd do what Jack Marriner would have done, if there'd been a photograph and he thought Pippa had it. I've been trying to set a trap for you for days, though I didn't know it was you I was trying to set it for. This evening I was sure this was the place to be.'

'May I inquire why?' asked Michael Craik politely.

'I saw somebody had shut this gate, shut the horses in this far paddock here. Who on earth would do that, and why? Completely pointless, unless there was a good reason. I could only think of one reason. I didn't think of it, actually, until I was already at home and getting my mother's tea. Then it came to me. I got my old gun out and jumped on my bicycle, and I was here before you. My mother will be very cross, being kept waiting for her tea.'

'I never saw you,' said Michael Craik, with a note of reluctant admiration.

'A-ben nobbut a titchy crawlen creetur, nex kin t'weasel,' said Dan.

'Weasel is right,' said another voice, a woman's voice. 'Drop that gun, Mallett.'

'Ah, Mrs Marriner, I was expecting you,' said Dan.

'Have you got a gun, Ju?' said Michael Craik, still on his knees on the ground with his knife on Pippa's neck.

'Yes, of course. I couldn't get at Jack's, so I went and got yours, as soon as I'd started the bonfire in that car.'

'Your timing there was spot on.'

'Good. It wasn't difficult. It was the last thing they were expecting. The car wasn't even locked.'

'Ye gotted yere gurt quick an' quiet,' said Dan admiringly to Judith Marriner.

'I've lived here most of my life. I know where to get through the hedges.'

'But you're in Italy!' squeaked Pippa suddenly from the ground.

'She never went to Italy. She never had the least intention of going to Italy,' said Dan. He whistled softly through his teeth, as though in admiring wonder.

The horses shifted and pricked their ears.

'But those telephone calls from Italy…'

'Who said they came from Italy? She said so. You heard a few clicks and buzzes, I expect, and somebody in the distance singing *O Sole Mio*. You knew quite well Mrs Marriner had gone to Italy. Why else were you here? Everybody in the world was perfectly certain she was in Italy. The telephone calls were just icing on the cake, really, to make certain everybody was certain she was a thousand miles away. Actually, I expect she was sitting in a motel five miles away.' Dan whistled again, amazed, awestruck. Cavendish and Dorothy both moved a yard towards Dan, and Talisman stopped grazing and raised his head.

'I knew my colleague would be along,' said Michael Craik over his shoulder to Dan. 'That's why I kept you talking. Ju darling, keep your gun pointed at Mallett. I'll do what's needed here. Then we'll dispose of Mallett. If we make any noise, they'll think it's the horses. It's pretty dark now; they won't see us against this jungle. Everything okay? Time to proceed?'

Pippa lay uncomfortably on the prickly ground under the hedge. She was very cold and frightened. From the corner of one eye she could see that the sky was black in the east; from the corner of the other she could see in the west luminous bands of acid green, which still gave a hint of dramatic visibility to the scene. The fire in the yard had subsided, and with it the shouts of the policemen. Now owls could be heard crying as they hunted at the edge of the woods, and there were tiny sounds of life clicking and buzzing in the depths of the hedge.

'Carry on, darling,' said Judith Marriner, telling her lover to cut Pippa's throat. Her voice was cold and brisk, unemotional, bored, impatient, bossy. Her tone was exactly as it had been when she gave Pippa her instructions, before any of this had begun... Except that, of course, it had already begun. Judith Marriner was spreading round London the news that she was about to go to Italy. Pippa had overheard. That was why Pippa, and not some other, was lying under this hedge.

'You have to hand it to them,' said Dan. 'No, wait, I must pay this tribute.'

Pippa thought he was making time. Michael Craik might have realized this too, but he held his hand because he was vain, because he wanted to hear Dan's tribute to his cleverness.

Dan whistled. His whistle expressed amazement to Michael Craik and Judith Marriner, but it expressed a summons to the horses.

'The real murderer,' said Dan, 'is somebody that everybody knows is in Italy, and the one everybody thinks is the murderer is actually at the bottom of the English Channel, and has been for three years. Great trick. It's almost a pity that it didn't work.' Dan whistled.

'But it did work,' said Michael Craik.

Pippa, from the ground, from the drift of dead leaves which pillowed her head, could see against the sky the horses almost on top of them. They were darker shapes silhouetted against the darkness. She would not have seen them, she thought, from any other position. She knew Dan knew they were there, because he had called them, because he could see in the dark.

'Gum,' said Dan, his voice bubbling with slow misery through molasses. 'A-ben beated t'runnocks by grander brainses.'

'I don't know what runnocks are,' said Judith Marriner, 'but I'd say you're exactly right.'

Pippa saw that the big Cavendish was now very close to them. His forefeet, nervously shifting, were not two yards from her head on the ground under the hedge, his head not a yard from Michael Craik's. The old mare Dorothy was beside and just behind him, on the side away from Pippa and nearer to Judith Marriner. Pippa could not see Talisman, but she knew he was just behind the other two. More than a ton of bone and muscle almost overhung the frail little group of humans in the corner of the field. The horses had been drawn almost into the group by Dan's seductive whistles.

The horses thought they were going to be given lumps of sugar.

Dan had known the horses, and they Dan, all their lives. No doubt he had always dealt honestly by them. When he called them, and they came, they were rewarded. They trusted him. Over the years, Dan had been good to these gentle and sinless animals, which had been despised by their owner who had inherited them. The notion blazed like a comet through Pippa's head: the horses are going to repay Dan's kindness.

Even as she tried to comfort herself with this childish idea — even as she felt the prick of the needle-sharp knife-point on her neck, as she sensed impatience in the burly dark figure looming above her — a violent commotion exploded in the near-darkness four yards away. Somebody — it must have been Dan — rocketed like a driven pheasant out of the fringe of the hedge, into the flank of the tall horse Cavendish. Cavendish gave a whistle of astonishment and buck-jumped into the air. The blackness was now full of bedlam, shouting, violent movement, collisions, a scream. Pippa dizzily realized that it was Judith Marriner's scream as the old mare Dorothy was knocked sideways by Cavendish into Judith.

Michael Craik's attention was distracted. Anybody's would have been. A statue would have been distracted, at that moment. The knife-point wandered from Pippa's neck. Michael Craik himself gave a sudden grunt of astonishment, shock, agony. Pippa thought Cavendish had trodden on his leg. Pippa suddenly wriggled backwards along and under the hedge, scratching herself on thorns and brambles, inhaling wet dead leaves and ancient cobwebs. Judith Marriner screamed again, and there was a crash, a body crashing into a tangle of brambles in the dark, knocked into the hedge by a startled horse. A shocking explosion immediately followed, a gunshot. Pippa heard herself scream. Perhaps Judith had fired at Dan. Perhaps she had hit him. Against the sky Pippa could see the horses, black shapes on black. She saw them rear and bolt, panicked by the shot. She heard the hooves of the three horses thudding away across the paddock.

Pippa struggled to her hands and knees to be less helpless, to be able to jump up and run after the horses if that seemed a good thing to do. She was praying that Michael Craik could not see her, and that Judith Marriner had not shot Dan.

Suddenly, a long, narrow blue-white triangle slashed the darkness, the beam of a flashlight. The beam swung, wavered, and skewered Judith Marriner, who was floundering helplessly in a tangle of brambles in the hedge. There was a shotgun at her feet. She was wearing drab-coloured trousers and trainers and a Barbour jacket. She looked tousled and angry and terrified and helpless, like a beetle on its back.

A hand jumped down out of the darkness into the torch-beam. The hand picked up the double-barrelled shotgun. It was Dan's hand.

Dan said, 'Thanks.'

Pippa groggily thought: *he's holding the torch and he's holding his own gun and he's picked up the other gun. He's got three hands.*

Pippa understood that Dan had had no gun. He had lied. He had bluffed them. But now he had a gun.

The torch-beam wavered and groped and found Pippa, now struggling to her feet.

'All right, love?' said Dan gently.

'Yes,' said Pippa, and burst into tears.

The beam swung to Michael Craik, who was crouched on the grass, clutching his knee and groaning. The knife was on the ground beside him. He had forgotten about it. It was no longer any use to him at all.

'Cavendish put his foot down a mite clumsy,' said Dan. 'I didn't think he'd tread on you. I'm thankful he didn't.'

'So am I,' sobbed Pippa.

More feet now thudded over the grass towards them, many more lights. The police came, brought by the sound of the shot.

The police laid hands on Dan; then, realizing their mistake, they arrested Michael Craik, calling for a stretcher on which he could be carried off into custody. They pulled Judith Marriner out of the hedge and arrested her.

'If Michael Craik had done what he intended,' said the Detective Chief Superintendent, 'if he had killed Miss Lees and left half a photograph on her body, of course we would have believed that Jack Marriner had killed her for the other half of the photograph, in which, of course, we would have continued to believe. We would have pictured Jack Marriner disappearing somewhere into continental Europe, into a prepared slot, an impenetrable ready-made disguise, from which, in the end, we would have expected to flush him. As Mallett says, we would have devoted all our energies to searching the wrong country.'

'Niver thinken t'sarch nearer t'home,' said Dan, 'niver loweren eyes t'local doens.'

'And the man we would have been looking for has been dead for three years.'

''Ose ben parls 'at were 'is eyes,' murmured Dan, causing the Superintendent to look at him in amazement, and Pippa to give a sudden and helpless wail of laughter.

Her laughter was slightly hysterical. She was on a high of thankfulness, after the imminent threat of death. She was so overflowing with grateful love she thought that, if she bent over, it would spill out.

'We imagine Mrs Marriner had a record, a tape, perhaps a video, to serve as the Italian background to those telephone calls,' said the Superintendent. 'She kept the calls extremely short, partly to give nothing away while not seeming unnaturally secretive, partly to make certain that the origins of the calls could not be traced. Latterly she might have guessed that we were prepared to trace any incoming call, so she rang the garage instead. That established, with total conviction, that she was still in Italy.'

'And of course nobody looked at her passport,' said Pippa, 'as nobody does anymore.'

'She did not use her passport, Miss Lees.'

'Oh. Nor she did. One gets muddled.'

'One does indeed. Now, it would be highly convenient for all parties, the police not least, if you would be so very kind as to stay here, Miss Lees. Mrs Marriner will be remanded in custody. Somebody must be here. Will you consent to continue to take care of the house and the animals? Have you pressing engagements elsewhere?'

'Um, nothing I can't postpone,' said Pippa.

'Will you stay, then, for the time being? Your salary, of course, will continue to be paid, and the household expenses met.'

'All right,' said Pippa, struggling to seem to be conferring a favour.

'I daresay Mallett will assist you with the horses, and any heavy tasks that require to be done.'

Dan gave a humble grunt. He touched his forelock, grossly overacting.

'We can remove ourselves immediately,' said the Superintendent, 'and leave you both in peace.'

At three o'clock in the morning, Pippa suddenly prodded Dan in the ribs.

He mumbled and rolled over to face her.

'What did that damned policeman mean,' said Pippa, '"We'll leave you *both* in peace"?'

'He meant you and Mr Tomkins,' said Dan. 'Go back to sleep.'

'What are "runnocks"?'

'Never heard of them.'

'Yes you have. You said to Judith Marriner that you'd been beaten to runnocks by grander brainses.'

'Did I say that? I wonder what I meant. It's a new word to me. I must have made it up.'

'Oh Dan, you are a monster.'

'A smallish monster.'

'You've beaten me to runnocks,' said Pippa adoringly, and they began to make love again to the cry of the distant owls.

A NOTE TO THE READER

Dear Reader,

If you have enjoyed this novel enough to leave a review on **Amazon** and **Goodreads**, then we would be truly grateful.

Sapere Books is an exciting new publisher of brilliant fiction and popular history.

To find out more about our latest releases and our monthly bargain books visit our website: **saperebooks.com**

www.ingramcontent.com/pod-product-compliance
Lightning Source LLC
Chambersburg PA
CBHW060435180626
46817CB00007B/2824